Grandma Anna
and Me 1853

Grandma Anna and Me 1853

A Book on
Wisdom - Teaching - Learning

Nancy L. B. Vaughan

iUniverse LLC
Bloomington

GRANDMA ANNA AND ME 1853

iUniverse books may be ordered through booksellers or by contacting:

iUniverse LLC
1663 Liberty Drive
Bloomington, IN 47403
www.iuniverse.com
1-800-Authors (1-800-288-4677)

Because of the dynamic nature of the Internet, any web addresses or links contained in this book may have changed since publication and may no longer be valid. The views expressed in this work are solely those of the author and do not necessarily reflect the views of the publisher, and the publisher hereby disclaims any responsibility for them.

Any people depicted in stock imagery provided by Thinkstock are models, and such images are being used for illustrative purposes only. Certain stock imagery © Thinkstock.

ISBN: 978-1-4917-2171-1 (sc)
ISBN: 978-1-4917-2172-8 (e)

Library of Congress Control Number: 2014901188

Printed in the United States of America.

iUniverse rev. date: 03/05/2014

Unless indicated, Bible quotations are taken from the King James Version of the Holy Bible.

NancyytVaugh@aol.com

Contents

SECTION IV

SECTION V

SECTION VI

In Memory of my Son
Russell Clay Bryson
January 4, 1962-January 27, 2007

Contents

The memories of my ancestors were strong influences in the writing of this book based on their lives. The hardships they endured and the courage of themselves and others

The events that have taken place in this book are like recycling, they all have taken place somewhere in time, with other peoples, in other places I am sure. This book however, will serve as a catalyst for us to recall as many actions as we can, strive not to forget them, because they are our history. Preserving them for our children and their children's children, from generation to generation. Priceless, precious memories that must be remembered and preserved.

Just as Jesus gave us the Lord's Prayer as a model to use in praying, this book of events that were experienced by many slave families are models, the only difference being, the names of those who have had these experiences. From the old ones, the long ago gone ones, we have inherited a rich heritage of perseverance and survival.

Their experiences and survival skills should be a vital pattern, inspiring us to read and appreciate the legacies they left. These should be used as building blocks and patterns for our life's journey.

"Grandma Anna and Me 1853" explores the relationship with our past that has impacted our present.

It is designed to be read by adults as well as children. Reading it to the younger generation will inspire them to discuss the stories among themselves and with others. Encouraging them to create their own drawings enhances and stretches their imaginations. The quizzes and research projects on the Bible will encourage research, which within itself expands learning and knowledge.

Seek out older persons you know who have drunk deeply from the cups of wisdom, love, kindness, forgiveness and understanding throughout their lives.

The wisdom they share with you will help. "So you might flourish and grow in your faith."

Psalms 92: 10-14

Acknowledgments

The author wishes to acknowledge the generous and expert contributions of those who provided us with images and historical information. Edna Reah Vaughn, Assistant Liberian First Baptist Church 200 East Main, Tom Brown historian First Baptist Church 200 East Main, Murfreesboro, TN, Rutherford County Archives, First Baptist 738 East Castle Street, and the members of my family. Unless otherwise indicated, all Scripture quotations are taken from the NIV of the Holy Bible.

Section I

Strong Influences

True life stories bring vivid, inspiring memories to strong life teaching. Strong teaching must first be taught, in order for it to be leaned. To deliver strong teaching one must have strong teachers. Down through the generations we all have at one time of the other, experienced strong teachers in our lives, such as the woman of whom I write, my Grandma Anna. Welcome readers to her world of wisdom, and the lessons she taught our family.

These are the stories told as seen through the eyes of a twelve-year old relative of mine many generations past. These are stories and incidents that make families remember all the oral family history stories spoken, some that were written on tiny scraps of paper tucked away, and yellowing in old cherished and worn family Bibles. Preserved down through the years they say, "Yes, to remember is the extension of your family's lifeline."

This is the story of a bonding and love between a Grandmother and Granddaughter many years ago. The young girl falls in love with the sense of awe and the wonders of the world as she learns them through the patience and limited teaching knowledge of her Grandma Anna. You might say to yourself "this is the story of a slave family!", I would answer you "yes, it is!" This is not the story of glamorizing the institution of slavery, which within itself was shameful, horrible, a dehumanization of a people. The practice should have ended years earlier. This however, is the story of how love is not chained by shackles, and cannot be broken through mistreatment. Love always holds fast. Love is the emotion that holds families together in spite of anything and everything else that is taking place in their lives. Love is invisible, you cannot touch it, but you can feel its presence. I will list some of the emotions of what love is, and some of the emotions that love is not, as told to me, Lucy Mae by my Grandma Anna. She would say Lucy Mae:

Love
Is
Giving
Kind
Long Lasting
Forgiving
Soft Spoken
Patient
Hope
Endurance but
The
Greatest of
These
Is
Love

Love
Is
Not
Mean
Selfish
Envy
Or
Backbiting
Negativity
Murder
And
Selfishness
If that
Comes Your
Way
Is
Not
Love

If you see any of dese my child, dat is not love cropping up in yo life Lucy Mae, dat be evil, so, change and change quickly, because dese are not of God . . . and certainly not de way love works. "Flee from dese things my child." "Run like the wind child."

Our Family

My name is Lucy Mae Mathis. The year is 1853. I will soon turn twelve years old. I have a very good family and we love each other. My Grandpa's name is Job. He is an old man full of experience and has weathered many a storm and survived just as Grandma Anna has. My Grandpa Job at an early age was kicked by a stubborn mule he was trying to hitch to a wagon for hauling tobacco, that old mule kicked him in the side so hard it broke his leg and displaced his hip, leaving him walking for the rest of his life as if one leg is shorter than the other, plus he has to use a walking cane for support. He and Grandma Anna were married plantation style, where the Masa of the plantation just said, "You 'all married." They had quite a few children, but my Father Willie, was the only child they had to live to become a grown man. My father Willie married a girl that grew up on a plantation in Smyrna, Tennessee. Her name is Willie Mae. Grandma Anna said folks would sometimes just call "Willie" and they both would answer, which was sort of funny, so folks made it their business to always call her by her full name, "Willie Mae."

I have three brothers, Ruben, who is ten years old, Andrew, age seven and of course JW, who Grandpa Job calls the "runt," he is four years old.

We had a baby sister born in 1857 whose name was Olivia Mathis. She was still born, or as the old folks and family members would say "she transitioned before she came to earth."

Transition was just another word for "died." Seems like most folks just could not bring themselves to say the word "dead," they would say "crossed over", "transition" or, "gone on home," anything but died or dead. They said it sounded just too final, cause we not see them again here on dis earth, only at the judgment.

Eighteen fifty seven when Olivia died Pastor Nelson "Pappy" Grover Merry still be with us as Preacher for Bethel folks and any others that wanted to join the newly formed white First Baptist Church that had formed in 1843. The white First Baptist Church we have now was later given to the colored folks around 1859. We will never forget the death of Olivia, cause the day of her funeral was a sad day for the folks of Bethel. Olivia's dying and on that same day poor Pastor Merry being chased out of Murfreesboro by some white folks that never wanted him here anyway.

He came to Murfreesboro at the request of First Baptist Church elite white members, but some other folks just did not want a colored preacher in town.

Some white members of white First Baptist Church and some others white folks from the town of Murfreesboro (which had more saloons than they had churches) that they could get to side with them, kept a close watch on Pastor Merry, even to the point some folks say they were writing down all he did. Seeing as how the saloons in Murfreesboro outnumber the churches, was not really hard to get the local town drunks to join in and cause problems, many did not like black slaves anyway, so that be right up they alley to cause trouble, wanting to lynch somebody. Didn't want no uppity ex-slave here teaching and preaching.

The day we be having Olivia's funeral in the front yard of our cabin, lots of folks colors and whites be there watching, Sunday be the day we had her funeral.

Pastor Merry be preaching her funeral, folks crying, chillums eyes all stretched like they be saying, "what is happening?" Here come this crowd of white men, carrying whips, guns, ropes, sticks, rocks and whatever else they had that would cause harm, jumped poor Pastor Merry, beating, stomping, whipping, spitting, and screaming at him. White folks there for the funeral caught off guard, didn't know what to do! Just stand there. Colored folks be so scared, wit them guns pointed at them. JB tried to jump in to help Pastor Merry but somebody knocked him out cold with the butt of a gun. Poor Pastor Merry trying to run and get away, they be tearing his clothes off him, til he be buck naked! No clothes on at all! Somehow he manages to get away, running, falling, getting up, and running again. They say he showed up at the cabin of some colors who did not live at Cedar Grove, they gave him some clothes from what little they had, so he could get to Nashville. They say these folks that helped him, be so scared that someone gonna burn their home down, but that did not happen, we all thankful for that.

By that time Murfreesboro and surrounding areas had what they called roving preachers who went from place to place preaching, however most of these traveling Pastors had heard what had happened to poor Pastor Merry here in Murfreesboro, Tennessee so they were not in any hurry to fill his shoes. Pastor Copeland came and went. Pastor Copeland did not stay long enough for us to learn his first name. We go to church, some of the men Deacons lead songs we know and prayed, and this be our church services. I tell you all this now because all this happened between 1853 when Pastor Merry came to Bethel, and 1857 when these folks in Murfreesboro chased him away. Between these dates lots of other things happened, some funny, some sad.

My Mother Willie Mae named our sister Olivia Mathis. She said "she will always be a part of this family and that everybody needs a name." Grandma Anna had made her this pretty little white dress to wear the first Sunday we would have church, but that was not to be, instead that little white dress became her burial dress, a returning home to God dress.

I remember Olivia, she looked just like a baby doll, all dressed in her burial dress. I miss having a sister. There is just something about having a sister to share secrets and fun things with. Brothers are okay, but Sisters, awe! I miss her so much and the fun we would have had together. Seems to me like if my Mama had been able to rest some while she was carrying my sister, things might have turned out different, but in family way or not in family way every slave had a job to do and was expected to get it done, no if's, and's, or but's about it, so day after day Mama, body swollen, back and feet hurting, would drag herself up to the "big house." Grandma Anna used to say, "there ain't never no rest for de weary."

Papa, my brothers and me was working in the fields the day Mama had to come back to the cabin from work. Grandpa Job was sitting in the yard carving little round wooden marbles for my brothers to play with. Every once in a while he would look up and stare down the dusty road as he usually did like he expecting to see somebody a coming, this time he did see somebody a coming, but could not tell who it was.

"Anna, some body be a coming down the road headed this away, squinting her eyes, Grandma Anna got up and looked down the road as the figure drew near. "Oh Lawd Job, it be Willie Mae", off they tore a running down the road to meet her. Grandpa Job hobbling with his cane as fast as them cripple legs could carry him.

They caught Mama under each arm almost dragging her 'cause she could hardly walk. Helped her to the cabin and inside to lay down, by this time she was really hurting.

Grandma Anna told Grandpa Job to go get Aunt Grace, and Maude (who is deaf and dumb) but a good worker, to come help with this birthing. Grandma Anna could already see this birth was not going to be easy. The other Bethel women arrived as quickly as they heard and could get out of the fields or from the big house. Aunt Sadie came too, she was old and did not work the fields or the big house anymore, but she had all kinds of knowledge in that old grey head of hers.

As Papa, my brothers and me come in from working them baca fields Grandpa Job explained to us that Mama was ready to have the new baby. My little brothers jumped up and down clapping their hands, but they were clapping for a boy! They were wishing for a boy, a brother! Me? I had my heart set on a sister, no two ways about it.

What Grandpa did say that made me silently worry was that "Mama was real sick?"

Mama screamed, when she was not screaming, she was moaning, Aunt Grace, with her bossy self, told Grandpa to get some quilts and make pallets on the ground so we could get some sleep, but I knew very little sleep would I get.

To give Mama the privacy she needed at that time everyone, except those helping with the birth remained outside. It was the beginning of October, and in Tennessee at that time it is not very cold. Wrapping up good in the quilts warded off any little chill you might feel, so we waited and waited. Grandpa Job had built a fire under the wash kettle 'cause the birthing ladies needed hot water from time to time. The heat from the fire cut the slight chill, plus just lying there watching the sparks pop up from the burning wood seemed to settle my nerves some. And so we waited and waited, like Grandma Annie would say "seemed just like time just stood still." Suddenly we heard a loud scream "Oh Lawd naw." We all set up looking at one another. Slowly Grandma Anna come out to tell us the terrible news, Olivia did not make it. My poor Papa fell apart! Sadness comes, but what slave has not experienced sadness? It is a part of life. Soon we will be done with the troubles of this world! Olivia would see no trouble of this world, she gone back home. I drew the blanket up over my head and cried, nobody bothered me, they knew this was my private time.

Names

I guess after the death of Olivia, I decided names were important. A name is what you answer to for the rest of your life, but in our family and the community of Bethel we have some strange names. Some folks liked their names, others just hated their names and sometimes would not answer to that name. Sometimes seems to me look like the names actually fit the descriptions of the person. Take for instant our great Aunt Snow. She seemed to like her name and her name seemed to fit her, seeing as how she was very fair skinned, a mulatto.

Tennessee was a cousin of ours, call her "Tennessee" and you had a fight on your hands. She did not claim it, did not answer to it. Would tell you very quickly her name was "Tennie." Of course all official slave papers had to have "Tennessee" on them, but in her official mind it remained "Tennie" period!

My Great Great-Great-Grand mother's name was Narcissus. Guess she was satisfied with her name seeing as how she was named for a "flower."

Then there was Uncle Big Bub, to this day I have never heard anything other than "Uncle Big Bud." What his real name was I never knew!

Aunt Lovie, Grandmother Nancieanne, Magnoila, Gussie Bell, Iona (African name meaning "I own her") Lady, cousin J Bird, Sister Hollie hawk, Mr. Limb, Mr. Skipper, Two Mr. Bucks, Mr. Nute, Miss Willow, and don't forget Pastor Merry, Aunt Hen, Mr. Bude, Uncle Opie, Flossie, Texanna, Aunt Nubian, King George, Mindy, Luke, Miss Lindy, and Spring. There were other names that were different, but all these folks were a part of the community of "Bethel," which within its self, had a special meaning in its name to all of us.

Our Location

We worked on a plantation in southeast Rutherford County, Murfreesborough, Tennessee. Grandma Anna said it used to be called Cannonsburgh but that lasted only one week and when Nuton Cannon rewrote the document that named this location Cannonsburge that line was left out, was not in there. Might have been shamed of his self for trying to name a town after his own self. In 1811 they changed the name to Murfreesboro, Tennessee and for a while they said it served as the capital of Tennessee. Grandma Anna said in 1826 Nashville became the capital of the state of Tennessee because the Governor did not want to live in Murfreesboro.

Murfreesboro is the direct center of Tennessee.

Slavery in Tennessee and how it operated depended on what part of Tennessee it was.

There was slavery in East Tennessee, but the numbers were small in East Tennessee. The struggling white settler, if he had a slave, they worked hand-in-hand with each other. East Tennessee was a mountainous area, not suitable for massive acres to raise cotton, tobacco and corn. Small farmers and their slaves had more direct association.

Middle Tennessee, had larger estates than East Tennessee, Stones River for transportation, therefore, the numbers of slaves were larger than East Tennessee, but not West Tennessee. West Tennessee with that flat land, the Tennessee River and the Great Mississippi River used for transportation made cotton growing successful, and required large numbers of slaves to cultivate the land and cotton.

Slaves who came from west Tennessee into middle Tennessee after being sold to a Middle Tennessee slave holder were greatly surprised at the treatment they received from their owners. Tennessee, they said, had laws to protect the treatment of slaves. If they were used or not, is not recorded in history, but at least Tennessee put them in her Tennessee law. Some Master's did, others didn't, depending on they attitude toward colors.

The community we lived in was a slave community called "Bethel." Bethel was located in Southeast Rutherford County (Murfreesboro) TN. Some other folks say Bethel was located as you traveled out the Bradyville Pike toward Woodbury Tennessee. Others say it was located near where First Baptist Church was located near Sevier and Springs Streets, other folks say it be closer to an area called the "bottoms." I don't know our exact location, just know I'm here.

Some of the slaves that lived in Bethel worked the surrounding plantations of which they were a part of. They walked to their jobs, or they were hauled by wagons, colored overseers usually drove the slaves to and from the various locations. White overseers watched the field work of slaves and patrolled the roads for anyone that might want to take the chance of running away.

My family worked on a plantation owned by Masa John and Missus Sarah Mathis.

That's how our name comes to be Mathis. Slave families took the names of their owners.

The name of the plantation we lived on was called "Cedar Grove" because of all the cedar trees that grew there. Those cedar trees came in handy, all the wood was used for heating and building.

Grandma Anna

Grandma Anna was a medium built woman, not very tall, but strong as any man when it came to doing work. She had learned as a young girl, keep your mouth shut, and do the work expected for you to do, at least try. That way you avoided fewer punishments, from anyone that might have been in control of you that might have had a bad day. Grandma Anna had become too old to do hard physical work in the "big house" so she used the knowledge her Mother had passed on to her about secret receipts on how to make herbal medicines to cure plantation owners, as well as slave families, when they became ill. There were medical doctors but many times they were unable to come to the plantation when there was an emergency, therefore Grandma Anna's skills were used. She could set a broken ankle, foot, arm, and leg as good as any old Doctor could. In fact she set Grandpa Job's leg and hip, the best she could, when that old mule had given him a nasty injury. She was just a young girl then and he a young boy, later they became husband and wife as I have stated earlier. Both were slaves on plantation "Cedar Grove."

She was also what they called a "midwife," a female who helped the ladies when they went into labor to deliver their babies. Sometimes the white women had to use the skills of Grandma Anna to deliver their babies, just depended if the medical Doctor could get there in time or not. The road, when it was raining, and icy conditions, or snow, many times caused travel problems. It is so wonderful to see folks improve from their sickness because of the help Grandma Anna gave them. Some folks trusted her medicine practice more than they did the doctor.

Grandpa Job

Grandpa Job had become too old to work the fields too. Grandpa Job was a tall slender man. The hair he had on his head was turning grey and his head was balding. As he got older, his eyes were beginning to have a bluish color to them. Some of the other older man looked like that to. Grandma Anna said they eyes were getting weak. She said a coat of skin begins to overcast they eyes giving them appearances of having blue-gray eyes.

Grandpa walked with a limp cause of an accident he had as a young man. There was always other work he had to do, like planting a garden, raisings hogs, building fires for the big house in the winter, early spring and late fall when the weather still had a chill in the air.

And doing something he really did not like doing, but could not say "no" too, and that was shining old Masa shoes! He hated that! He would do that crazy little grin when he was disgusted, and say "yes Sir, will be like new shinning brass Sir!" Masa John look like he going to hand them shoes to Grandpa Job, but when Grandpa Job would reach to take them from his hand, Masa would drop them to the ground and laugh. Masa John would laugh and laugh and laugh, saying, "Just thought I'd give you a little exercise Job old boy." Poor Grandpa Job smiling and grinning, would stoop over as best he could, cause of his cripple condition, and pick dem shoes up, saying to him, "yes Sir, I get these done real shiny for you Sir!" When Masa John left Grandpa Job would be as mad as a wet hen, he would just shake his head.

Grandma Anna would just say to him, "Soon be over wit Job." He would say to Grandma Anna "ought to shine his own shoes, dey his feet, dey his shoes, dey his smelly shoes, not mine". "Masa John just devilish" Grandpa said. Grandpa Job and Grandma Anna both got a good laugh. Laughing seems to make any situation more bearable, or at least it seemed like it did.

Questions, Questions

Before I turned twelve years old I would beg Grandma Anna to teach me her Mama and Grandma's secrets, and she would smile and say, "wait until you turn twelve years old Lucy Mae, den I will teach you," then she would always gave me a gentle kiss right in the middle of my forehead.

I loved to see her beautiful brown eyes looking at me tenderly. My Grandma Anna was so special to me and I loved her dearly.

Before turning twelve years old, I could hardly wait for what she called the "magic number twelve" she was going to tell me about. When I did turn twelve January 4, 1853, it seemed like forever before she made her mind up to teach me all she knew about "twelve" and many other things I wanted her to tell me about, or a part of it. I really have a lot to learn.

I asked Grandma Anna why she called the number " twelve" a magic number?

She said, "Child dat number has to be special because of the number of times God used dat number in his planning of creation and in the Bible," but I'll tell you all about that later.

I would think to myself, but I would not dare say it out loud, Here we go again with, "I will tell you later." Looks like later be never!

Section II

Tell Me about Us

Grandma Anna explained that many years ago ancestors of our family lived on an entire continent named Africa. She always referred to Africa as "Motherland" when telling the oral stories she had heard down through the years from family members.

Grandma Anna said her great-great-great Grandma recalled being put on a ship in Africa, carried through "The Middle Passage," landing in the Caribbean, and then put on a boat that eventually landed at a place called Memphis, Tennessee. Memphis was the slave-trading center of the Mid-South. "Buy more slaves to raise more cotton, to buy more slaves, to raise more cotton!" That was the way the cycle worked. The entire system was like a circle that looked like it would never be broken. She said she later learned that Nashville, Tennessee ran a close second to Memphis in the buying and selling of human beings.

She said when they put her on the slave block to be sold, she was so afraid. Her Mama, Papa, brothers and sisters were all sold separately, which meant she was just a lonely scared teenage girl.

She say she remembered Masa John's Great-Great-Grand Pappy and many other white men walking around her looking her over to see if she had any defects that would cost them money to fix.

"I manage to look up once in a while when they were inspecting me." Grandma said she had always been told not to look up, just keep your head lowered. She did look up, and looked directly into the eyes of Masa John Great-Great-Grand Pappy, "he smiled at me, and I saw in his eyes a kindness that I failed to see in the eyes of the other men," she said. I thought to myself, "If this man buys me maybe I will not have to face such a hard time in life."

I quickly looked away, and the bidding started, seems like it lasted forever. I finally heard the "barker man" calling all the bids, saying" sold for $700.00 to Planter John Mathis from Rutherford County, Tennessee.

Thus begins the long trip in the back of a wagon, then on a boat, with wide railings that white folks called a ferry to Cedar Grove Plantation.

We crossed what they say was the Tennessee River and eventually arrived in Rutherford County Tennessee.

Great-Great-Great Grandma learned, by paying attention that the life of the Tennessee slave in many instances were not as hash as many other places.

Tennessee had a slave code that guaranteed slaves, shelter, food, clothing and medical attention. If a slave grew old like Grandma Anna and Grandpa Job and could no longer work, they were taken care of in their old age. Laws were on the books concerning treatments, but it all depended on the attitude of the slave owners as to how their slaves were treated. Many never heard of these laws, if they did, they show didn't pay them no attention. Many a slave's back has been cut to shreds of bleeding skin, for something as simple, as looking overseers and owners straight in the eye.

From this single, alone, lost, scared young girl came a generation of her descendants, me being one of them.

Grandma Anna always said no matter where you came from, every slave lost the most important thing in the world to them, "They freedom." That was the most important thing they could have ever lose, even more precious than their very lives, their history being forever, lost, strayed or stolen."

To be suddenly ripped away from everyone and everything you have ever known. A beautiful land, sometimes being a part of royalty leaving your relatives and friends. Leaving a life style that you were used to and where you felt safe. This uprooting literally turned the world of the captured slave upside down, causing complete confusion and misery.

Slavery divided parents, children, husbands, and wives were separated, never to see each other again. These were heartbreaking memories for Grandma Anna as she told these stories of our past to me and my brothers.

Human cargo packed in the hull or belly of a ship, one common thread holding them all together, "iron chains." People, like clusters of grapes held together by one common vine, a chain, naked, half naked, afraid, confused, sick, lying in their own urine, vomit, feces, not understanding the language that was being spoken to them, total darkness day and night, due to windowless prisons where slaves were held before boarding the ships, and complete darkness in the hull of the ships. Allowed out once a day, just to be feed, and washed down with buckets of ocean water thrown on them. Ocean water 'cause of its salt content, was said to have helped in the healing of any sores or boils that the slaves suffered from. Many captured slaves jumped over board to escape this misery. Grandma Anna said that is where the song "Before I'd be a slave I'll be buried in my grave and go home to my Lord" came about, but at that time the song was sung by slaves in their native dialect. Later those same words were sung in English, but they still held the same meanings for the enslaved ones.

Any talking among the slaves that came from the same area and spoke the same dialect was not tolerated. The biting whips against bare backs put a stop to that.

But in they own language the slaves called the ships "ships of shame." These whips would leave scars that every slave would carry with them to their graves. Slaves were forced to learn English, no matter how crude their English was, that was what they had to learn to speak

Grandma Anna said "A higher power had to be looking and watching over all dem slaves, no matter where dey came from and whatever language dey speak, dey were all in the same situation, "deys all slaves."

Slave markets were where slaves were brought to be sold to the highest bidder, families were sold to different buyers, and children were purchased to play with the plantation owner's child, children or Grandchildren, "as a playmate." If that slave child was sold separate from his or her mother and father, a slave family on the plantation where the child was sold to, made that child a part of their family, that way the child did have someone to love and care for them, not kin by blood, but kin by love.

Slaves were field hands, house maids, wet nurses, male house servants, carpenters, overseers, blacksmiths, tailors and whatever else that might have been needed for them to do. The hardest job was being a field hand, and the hardest part of a slave woman was being a female! Some slaves with special skills were even hired out to work for others by their owners. Some of these slaves were allowed to keep the money they earned, others were not. Masa decided on dat!

Before Day Break Prayer Meetings

Slaves were gradually introduced to organized religion very early, and were forced and encouraged to attend white religious services. Being exposed to something they heard the religious leaders call "prayer meetings," slaves learned to create their own version of "prayer meetings." Any opportunity the slaves had to slip away deeply into the woods for "before day break prayer meetings" they did so.

They learned the routine of the overseers. They knew he could not work watching slaves all day and all night too. He had to sleep sometime.

Grandma Anna said three o'clock in the morning was the slipping away time. A watch person was left behind. The person who stayed behind had to watch and listen for anything. That person would make a sound like a common animal to that area, to warn the others if for some reason an overseer had heard or suspected something and came a looking. The slaves had learned a method of running in circles, that is, they never ran head on toward the overseers, they would scatter and would run toward the outside circling around the overseers. While the overseers were running into the middle of the meeting place, the slaves were running out and around the overseers. No two "before day break prayer meetings" were ever held in the same place twice Grandma Anna said.

These "before day break prayer meetings" was a time to sing long remembered native songs. Some slaves had practiced the Islam or Muslim faith, others West-African beliefs and practices, many others were forest and nature worshippers, so their worship became a mixture of the old and the new, what they remembered from the motherland and the God that the preacher man talked about as they listened on Sundays in the balcony of the First Baptist Church.

Grandma Anna was a very smart woman, although she could not read nor write, she had a keen ear for listening and paying attention to everything. She always prayed for wisdom. God must have heard her prayers and answered them, she was truly a wise woman, and it was always said people in Bethel loved and respected her, and even the white community respected her! Everyone calling her "Mama Anna."

I Do Not Understand Grandma Anna

Sunday morning was always the time slaves were required to attend the plantation owner's church. The way I figured as a little girl, this was just an extension of the learning process for slaves, if you are exposed to something long enough, you have a tendency to remember what you have heard or seen. If you felt the spirit and wanted to join First Baptist Church, when Preacher man opened the church for membership, you just go down from the balcony to the first floor and tell them so. You would be taken to a different part of Overall Creek or either Lytle Creek (Which were the town creeks) and they would baptized you. When First Baptist Church (white) gave their old First Baptist Church to us (colored) after they built a new church. Some of those that had been baptized as younger men and women slaves became the original founders, leaders(Deacons and Trustees), and members of First Baptist Church (colored) on the corner of Spring and Sevier Streets. Folks like, Alfred Hall, Harry Jordan, William Slancle, Dick Gentry, Rreuben Ransom, Stephen Dickinson, Henderson Hall, George Allen, Maryland Jordan, Dave Maney, Solomom Thompson, and John Oaff.

Some free colors lived in an area of Murfreesboro called "the bottoms." First Baptist Church was built on higher ground, but the land sloped down further down the street, and that area was the beginning point of the "bottoms," which flooded from the overflow of the town creeks every time there was a heavy rain. Poor folks having nothing know how, just standing there watching all their "nothings" float away. Misery! Mercy Lawd!

The church we attended had balconies, these areas were where the slaves sat.

There was a huge pipe organ that everyone loved to listen to. The organist always played beautiful music while folks were entering the sanctuary. After folks were settled in Pastor Eaton lead the congregation in singing hymnals.

The pastor was Pastor Joseph Haywood Eaton. Pastor Eaton was thirty-one years old when he became the first full time pastor of white First Baptist Church. It was rumored that he and the deacons of the church, Masas James Franklin Fletcher, Burrell Gannaway, Cyrus Smith, and John Molly had been discussing with Pastor R.B.C. Howell, Pastor of white First Baptist Church Capitol Hill in Nashville, Tennessee about bringing a colored preacher into our community of Bethel to have religious services held in our own community once a month. Seems as if this young man they were considering had been willed to Pastor Howell and his Capitol Hill church group by Misses Merry before she passed away. She wrote that in her will. The boy's name was Nelson Grover Merry, he had returned to Sumner County with Misses Merry. Masa Merry had died in Virginia where they lived. Misses Merry not wanting to live in Virginia far away from her folks came home to Sumner County to be near her kin. Her family was friends of the pastor at First Baptist Church Capitol Hill, Nashville, Tennessee. So off went Nelson, at sixteen years old, to Capitol Hill Nashville where he became the sexton of the church, which meant he be the janitor. Being a very smart person, Nelson caught on quickly to everything. The pastors of First Baptist Capitol Hill taught him to read and write, which at that time was against the laws of all of the states in the United States.

Our family attended white First Baptist church cause our owners attended there, but never thought we'd have a colored preacher man to come to Bethel though, we'd just wait and see. Might be folks just running they mouths.

We had this boy in Bethel named JB, he was the same age as me, he heard them (the white folks) talking about this, and he got busy spreading the news to us colors. Everybody (but not us), especially the white folks thought JB was touched in the head, meaning they though he was just plain "crazy". Uh huh! JB not crazy, he pulled them foolish acts to make them overseers think he was crazy, that way if he ran away from working in the fields, they would say "oh, that's just JB, don't waste time chasing him, he is as crazy as a loon!" Had all dem white folks fooled! That boy not "touched," "that boy crazy like a fox," yea! A real smart fox!

Grandma Anna used to say to JB, "Boy, I be scared for you, you take to many chances, one these days dese here white folks gonna learn your game, and you gonna be in real big trouble," and you know what he would say to Grandma? "Miss Anna, they gotta catch me first, I run to fast for dem old men," then bend over laughing, and slapping his legs! Grandma Anna would just shake her head, but she warned my brothers "don't follow dat boy nowhere, I mean dat, not nowhere! To dangerous!"

The hair on JB's Mama's head was snow white, and she was not old either! Same age as Willie Mae, my own Mama. Grandma Anna said, "JB put every one of dem gray hairs in his Mama's head." She said, "That boy was gonna be the death of his Mama." She stayed so worried 'bout him, she know he was not crazy and sooner or later them overseers gonna figure it out too, then he gonna be in big trouble. Enough about JB for right now, I'll tell you more about him later.

While we were in church I loved to lean against the balcony and watch the people downstairs file in and take their seats. Ladies in the fancy hooped dresses all trimmed in lace, wearing bonnets or hats, carrying purses, fans, and wearing gloves, speaking and bowing their heads to one another in little whispers. Grandma Anna called these outfits "Their Sunday Go to Meetings Dress." Little girls looking like miniature copies of the adult women, but just plain uncomfortable in all that get up go "Sunday Go to Meeting Dress." I looked down at the loose fitting colorless garment I had on, and a smile came to my face, because I bet they would have given anything to have on my loose garment rather than the ones they had on.

My friend Sarah, Masa John's Granddaughter looked up towards the balcony, saw me, and sneaked a little wave at me. I got ready to return the wave, but Grandma Anna very gently pushed my hand down, I looked at her, she shook her head.

The little boys were miniature copies of the men in their dress . . . . stocking, shoes, short pants fitted at the knees, course the men had on long pants though, the boys had little fitted black coats, stiff little white shirts, and a tie on their necks, as if it was chocking them, tight fitting little caps on their heads, which they had been taught to remove before entering the church or any house.

Bet they would have gladly exchanged their clothes for the freedom fitting clothes my little brothers had on.

Speaking of caps, someone had given my oldest brother Ruben a cap with a short bib to wear, he and that cap fell in love with each other, you would think that cap was glued to his head, he even slept in that cap. He asked Grandma Anna if he could wear it to church?. She said "yes, but remove it when you go in church." He said "yes ma'am," bounced in church with that cap on his head as if to say "Hey everybody, look at my cap." Grandma Anna tried to catch his eye, but he kept avoiding looking at her.

She always told us if we saw her blink her eyes really fast, we were doing something wrong and to stop it, so he knew what she wanted. Like a flash of lightning, just that quick, Grandma Anna reached over me, snatched that cap off Ruben's head so fast, my brother did not know what had happened. He sat there half scared, half mad, and not to surprised, because he knew what he had done. Grandma Anna finally caught his eye, blinked twice very fast. Neither of us saw that cap anymore. Ruben might have wanted to ask Grandma Anna about his cap, but he was too scared to do that, might get a late butt whipping!

After singing several hymnals, reading scriptures from the Bible, Preacher man takes his place in the pulpit to preach his sermon for that day. He begins to read, and I begin to listen:

> To everything there is a Season
> A time to every purpose under the heaven;
> A time to be born and a time to die;
> A time to plant, and a time to pluck up that which is planted;
> A time to kill and a time to heal;
> A time to break down and a time to build up;
> A time to weep, and a time to laugh, a time
> to mourn, and a time to dance;
> A time to cast away stones and a time together stones together;

A time to embrace; and a time to refrain from embracing;
A time to get, and a time to lose;
A time to keep, and a time to cast away;
A time to rend and a time to mend;
A time to keep silent and a time to speak;
A time to love, and a time to hate;
A time of war and a time of peace.
Ecclesiastes 3: verses 1 through 3

I listened very carefully to what preacher read and what he teach, but I could not understand how it all fit together in the sermon and the meaning of the message, it had so many:

"A time for this and a time for dat."

Walking back to the cabin, I told Grandma Anna I did not understand what it all meant. She said she would try and explain, to the best of her understanding, what he had said while we were preparing food for all of us to eat, which usually was not very much. Kusk, bacon, molasses, and maybe butter roll for dessert. After we finished eating, she started talking about what we had heard.

She said "Child as I see it, the meanings be just like the seasons, things change from time to time, nothing stays the same, and this is not to say it has not been done before, just maybe in another place and at another time.

In the seasons, we have spring and summer months, that is when the crops for man and beast grow, sometimes they produce a lot, other times they produce just a little, but there is a lesson in that too, it teaches folks to be careful and not waste so much. That what is produced must be shared by folks, farm beast, wild animals, and birds must all share in the produced crops.

Winter is the season where nothing is planted and nothing grows, weather is to cold. The ground goes to sleep, the soil is enriched by the leaves that have fallen in the fall and when the soil awakens in the Spring it is ready for planting again, "Don't know if you have ever paid any attention or not Lucy Mae," "but notice from now on how Masa John rotates his crops around, the same crop is never planted in the same field back to back. That gives the soil time to rebuild itself with a crop that does not require so many nutrients from it." "Are you understanding a little better Lucy Mae?" "yes mam" I said. The land has a chance to heal itself, she said.

Now for the part that speaks about killing. Child, I don't think that means killing people at least I hope not, but killing animals that are to be used for food, and if you see that the number of the species you are killing getting smaller, don't kill any more of them, and give them time to replenish or build up their own kind. That be my understanding of it.

You will later on in your adult life Lucy Mae hear it told differently, maybe speaking of people, rather than animals. It is a sad thing when folks kill each other, but God has his own special ways of doing things. Some things are not for us to understand.

"Tearing down and building up?" Sort of like that old shed Masa John had your Grandpa Job and some of the other men tear down. That old shed was useless, and so a new one that could be used was built in its place. "Does that make sense to you Child?" Could also mean as I see it, that God tore down the old ways of worship he gave to Moses to use with the Hebrew people. The laws and rules were just too hard for them to keep. They were doing wrong while trying to do right, just confusing, and then sometimes they were just hard headed and stubborn, disobeying God. Therefore God came up with another way for folks to worship Him even those who were not Jewish. They would be able to worship the Son of God that he sent to the earth whose name is called "Jesus Christ." "Men no longer had to go to the Priest to have him pray for us, we now can pray to Christ directly, isn't that nice Lucy Mae?" The curtain in the Holy Tabernacle was torn from top to bottom to give us direct conversion with Christ.

I asked, "Grandma who say the curtain in the temple be torn from top to bottom?" She said, "Pastor Eaton say it was said in the bible, that curtain, it was four feet thick, so no one on this here earth could claim they had torn it apart, only God had done this. Folks always be trying to take credit for what God did, like he need they help or something!"

We, Lucy Mae pray to Jesus Christ through the Holy Spirit, which is the part of God himself that he left with us for comfort. Remember when the Preacher said "Christ would never leave you nor forsake you?" "It is true today, now and forever Child." The Holy Spirit is the special person inside of us who lives with us daily and sees that God hears our prayers. He hears the prayers we pray, and then he sends those prayers straight to God himself."

There is a tale my Great Grandma used to tell me Lucy Mae when I was young like you and your brothers. She said, "The reason why every person has a dent in da top lip, is because before he or she is born, God places his finger dar, presses down lightly and says "shuuu," so we would never be able to speak and tell of all the beautiful things that we see in heaven before we came to earth."

"Now to crying and laughing, they are pretty much the same thing, there are tears of joy, full of happiness and laughter, and there are also tears of extreme pain, and sorrow over a loss. Such as a person transitioning, now that is sorrow, unless that transition is releasing him of suffering and pain. That is not laughter but it can bring a smile of relief from the suffering that person had endured, it is a relief for them."

"A time to dance! Remember the story of King David in the Bible, a man after God's own heart, he danced! He danced for joy for all the blessing and the forgiveness that God had granted him. David did a lot of wrong things, but he asked for forgiveness and God granted it. God knows we are not perfect people, so He gives us a chance to tell Him we be sorry for the wrong things we do, and ifn we mean it for true, He hears us and forgives us."

"Do you remember the story of King David preacher spoke about? I answered "yes ma'am I do."

"A time to move stones is like when you are building, or when you need stones for weapons. Like dat boy David, who was also a shepherd, that attended his Father's sheep (who later became King David). In the area where David watched his father's sheep there was a town that had terrible people that lived in it. They loves scaring and killing folks. Just to see which one was the most powerful in that area. This town they lived in was called Gath."

"The Philistines of Gath had been scaring the people of David's little town. No one wanted to fight Goliath the giant because he was too big, nine feet tall! Dat little old boy said, "I'll do it. Folks thought to themselves "dis little boy?" David gathered five rocks, his slang shot and took aim, shot that giant right between the eyes and dat rock hit so hard dat rock stuck in dat giant's forehead. Goliath had three brothers standing on the side line watching. When day saw what happened, they left so scared. So much for de good use of rocks and stones child. Dat was a time to dance and rejoice. Later on David when he was in battles with other folks used Goliath's sword. It had been given to him from the people cause da were so glad he had helped them get rid of dat mean old giant. Dat lil old boy was all grown up den and could handle that heavy sword."

"When we lost your baby sister Olivia, dat was a time to "cry", but when your brothers and de other Bethel boys threw baca worms at you, dat to them was a time to laugh, but not for you, it was a time for you to cry cause you was scared. What de situation is determines which you do, "laugh" or "cry". Feelings mean a lot in each one, crying or laughing. It is sometimes not easy to think of all the ways we are blessed daily."

"Casting away to me means, carrying all your problems to Jesus. He is the problem solver, always was, always will be. Just throw dem worries away from you and let the good Lawd solve them" she said. "He gonna be up anyway, Pastor say, "He neither slumbers or sleeps."

"Like Grandpa Job tears his pants, they now have a rip in them that I must repair, by sewing them back together because they had a rent or tear. Do not ever tear yourself away from de love of God, always make him first choice in your life."

"Opening your mouth to much by just talking all the time can cause you problems. Speak when spoken to. Baby Girl, God gave man two eyes, two ears, two holes in his nose to breath, and one mouth! Wonder why He gave just one mouth? Just imagine He wants us to see more, listen more, take a deep breath and talk less. Sometimes don't say anything at all, just remain silent. A closed mouth does not cause a problem for you or anyone else."

Now I thought to myself this would be the right time to ask Grandma Anna about the number "twelve" since she was explaining things and was in the mood to talk. So I just said "Grandma Anna tell me about "twelve" in Gods plans."

She said, "Numbers are important to God, so I'll just tell you about when de number twelve is spoken of. Ishmael, de son of Abraham by Haggai, who was Sari's maidservant, had twelve sons who became princes of a great nation, probably the Arab nations. Now here goes why "twelve" be so important."

Twelve

Jacob in de Bible had twelve sons

God divided de nation of Israel (his chosen people) into twelve sections, each of Jacob's twelve sons became the heads of those nations of Israel.

There were twelve stones in the ephod the Priest wore in the temple.

Twelve Minor Prophets

When building memorials to God twelve stones were used.

Jesus chose twelve men to become his disciples and apostles.

Heaven has twelve foundations.

Twelve planets, one on each gate of heaven

Twelve hours from midday noon to midnight

There are twelve divisions of heaven called the Mazzaroth.

There are twelve gates to the city of Zion.

Twelve fruits on the tree of life.

God made twelve months in a year

Twelve angels served as messengers

Truth is symbolized by 12 x 12

Jesus was twelve years old when He started His Ministry

Twelve represents divine authority, appointment, perfection, and completeness

The showbread for the temple had twelve loaves

Twelve Judges judged Israel

There were twelve baskets of food left after Jesus had fed nearly 5,000 people, like a big basket dinner, but more food!

There were twelve Patriarchs (Research the meaning of the word Patriarchs), write down what you find: _____

The Patriarchs were: Tell something about each person listed:

1. Shem
2. Arphaxad
3. Salah
4. Heber
5. Peleg
6. Reu
7. Serug
8. Nahor
9. Terah
10. Abraham
11. Isaac
12. Jacob

There were twelve people who were anointed (blessed) to serve in biblical government, they were (write a short description about each person listed)

1. Aaron
2. Nadah
3. Abihu
4. Eleazar
5. Ithamar
6. Saul* (Man's choice)

7. David* (God's choice)
8. Absalom
9. Solomon
10. Jehu
11. Joash
12. Jehoahaz

"Best we not forget all the benefits God has given to us" Grandma Anna said.

"A measure of good health, enjoyment of our families, the joy of knowing we have a heavenly Father, Lucy Mae, who cares for us."

"And dat we have the opportunity to serve Him, and we should."

"This is about as plain as I can make it child."

She asked me, "Baby Girl do all dis I am telling you make you understand?"

"Yes ma'am."

Research for you:

The priest wore in the Old Testament a garment called an ephod, that ephod had twelve gems stones sewed on it. Research these gems, locations where they are found today. Write a brief description of each one.

They were:

1. carnelian
2. Topaz
3. Smargd
4. Carbuncle
5. Sapphire
6. Emerald
7. Jacinth
8. Agate
9. Amethyst

10. Beryl
11. Onyx
12. Jasper

Grandma Anna prided herself on being able to remember things she hears. She always set quite when Pastor is preaching and teaching to the folks that attended. She always love when Pastor preached about Jesus and his twelve chosen men that followed him in his earthly work. She insisted that we learn all about the men called "disciples." know they names and something about them. We all had to listen and learn, me and my brothers, Grandpa Job, even my Mama and Papa too.

First we learn all dem names:

Simon Peter: Business man, Fishman, strong, short tempered, cursing man.
Andrew: Fisherman
James: Fisherman called "Son of Thunder", brother to John.
John: Fisherman "Son of Thunder", brother to James, suffered for his beliefs.
Philip: Fisherman from Galilee
Bartholomew: Probably a fisherman
Matthew: Tax collector
Thomas: called "doubting Thomas", had to see the marks in Jesus wrist. Did not believe anything unless he saw it for himself.
James: James "the lesser" to avoid confusion in the names of the other James.
Thaddeus: Fisherman
Simon: called the Zealot because of his furious beliefs
Judas Iscariot: The betrayer of Jesus, kept the money for the group
Matthias: The disciple who took Judas Iscariot's place after he hanged himself.

The same year 1853, that I turned twelve years old, Pastor Shelton, who had taken Pastor Eaton's place as Pastor of white First Baptist Church, he and the deacons of their church employed Nelson Grover Merry to preach to the colored members of the white First Baptist Church congregation in our own community, one Sunday a month. Nelson had been trained by R.B.C. Howell for the ministry and had been ordained in 1853 under Howell's direction. During the remainder of the time when he was not in Murfreesboro preaching, he preached to the colors of First Baptist Capitol Hill in Nashville.

His work in Murfreesboro called for a monthly Sabbath visits at which time he held prayer services in the homes of the Negro Baptist and delivered a sermon to the colors who were members in the afternoon at the First Baptist Church (white).

Everybody happy, clapping hands and bowing their heads when he be preaching. Young girls giggling, twisting around in the seats, and playing with their braids, all hoping to catch new Preacher's eye and maybe land they selves a husband.

Medicine Hunting

Grandma Anna kept her word to begin teaching me the many secrets of her herbal healing. She had a way of making work seem like play. She made it fun by exploring, hunting, and recognizing the plants that were nature's natural cures for illness. To hunt for the plants we would leave just at day-break going into the woods. Grandma Anna said the dew would have fallen on the plants and that would make them fresh for picking.

Lucy Mae," for every sickness dat man can and will ever have, God done put a cure for it in plants or animals. We just gotta to be smart enough to figure out what is what."

"This plant here is "Jerusalem oak seed" Lucy Mae. Put it in syrup or sugar water, let it sit for nine days, after nine days over give the chillum that have worms and stomach problems nine doses, one dose a day, the chillum who had worms will not have them anymore. All that butt scratching just stops!"

"Sage, lemon grass, watercress, mint, ginger, dandelion, and fever few" are just a few of the things I use" she said. Dese help wit colds and aches.

She also told me to watch to see what plants wild animals and birds ate, most of the times if animals and birds ate them and did not die, they were fairly safe for humans. I thought to myself, "suppose you don't see that the animal when he die, and you think it be safe, take it and then what?" In my mind I think, "Too bad, to sad, somebody might be calling the undertaker man!" However, those thoughts did not come out of my mouth. Leave well enough alone little girl, leave well enough alone!

A Big Boat Built on Dry Land

Grandma Anna said, "Seems like folks just don't know when to leave well enough alone." We knew when we was a sitting, resting and she had the time, she had one of her well-remembered Bible stories to tell all of us, and so we perked our ears for listening.

She said, "God had his reasons for making the world, animals and folks (Adam and Eve), but because of lies, not obeying, and the first murder, and the children of Adam and Eve just not controlling dey self. That Cain boy getting jealous and mad at he brother, led him to killing he brother Able. God just expelled the whole family from the Garden of Eden. He put an angel to guard the entrance so they could not reenter the beautiful garden, they would have tried to cause they didn't know anywhere else to go. No worry God had His plan, He told them where to go, with their heads hung low in sorrow they wondered out into the unknown. Cain paid a price for what he did, he was marked, and know man was allowed to kill him, God made him remember til his dying day what he had done. Adam and Eve had many children after that, enough to populate the whole entire world. But, as folks increased seems like all kinds of wrong doing increased as well. Folks just doing whatever they thought they could do, and would do, lying, cheating, killing, gambling, just everything!"

"God looked at the situation He has created and became upset and grieved with the whole thing" Grandma Anna said. God decided "I'll just kill off everything I created and start all over again anew."

You know chillum, "God always uses man to carry out his wishes, so God looked all over the world trying to find the right person to do his bidding, and seems like he weren't gonna be able to find no one."

God did not give up. He kept looking, finally in one little old evil town he found one good man and his family, that man's name was Noah. God came to Noah and explained to him what he intended to do, Can't say if Noah was happy or not, but we can say he was shore scared of them evil people in the towns around him and had to be careful not to get his wife, his three sons, their wives and his self hurt.

God explained to Noah that he wanted him to build a big boat, three stories high. He told him the kind of wood to use so it would float well, to put in one window and one door, and put a top or roof on the boat. "Go to the tar pits Noah and gather containers of tar pitch and seal the entire boat inside with the pitch, making it waterproof", so Noah did as he was told.

Runt broke in to ask "Grandma Anna how dey gonna breath in there all sealed up?" Her answer to him was, "If God has a will Baby Boy, he has a way for it to be done safely." Runt swollen hard, little eyes all big now, looking like he still be thinking, how that gonna be done? But he said nothing, just kept listening.

Well, Noah did exactly what God told him to do, folks in the town kept watching Noah, saying things to him like, "crazy man!, crazy man! Building a boat on dry land. Are you out of your mind? Or such things as, going fishing to catch some dry land terrapins? Can't eat them you know! So where you gonna fish at? Aint no such thing as rain! Noah never bothered to answer them about the reason for the building of the boat, but he did tell them how God was displeased with what they were doing, and he kept preaching to them to change they actions or they would be sorry. Grandma Anna said "they just kept on sinning."

Everyday more and more folks showed up to watch this out of his mind man build a big boat on dry land.

God had already told Noah what his plans were . . . to destroy, every living thing he had made except the ones he told Noah to bring into the boat with him and his family, male and female of each thing he brought inside the boat.

After a year the boat was complete, folks still poking fun at Noah, God made everything he had created, one male, one female crawl or walk into the ark together, Noah and his family bringing tons of food for humans and animals into the ark, took a long time for that to happen, but they finally finished!

God close the door himself, it started to rain, folks outside just thought it be a strange thing cause nobody had ever seem rain, the only wetness they ever see was the mist that arose up from out of the ground each day. That rain just would not stop! People begin to wonder what was happening, that much rain water was getting serious. Folks left outside started banging, clawing, cursing, and begging to get inside the boat, but boat kept on floating, folks kept pleading, rain kept on a falling! Water filled valleys, went over hills, and over mountains, finally everything just plain quite. Rain kept falling, forty days and forty nights.

Noah, his family and all the animals inside stayed in the boat for one year, Noah was 600 years old when he want in the ark, when he came out he was 601.

To find out if everything was safe, Noah sent a raven bird out, he did not come back. Later Noah sent out a little old dove, she came back cause she could not find a safe place to land, later Noah sent her out again, she brought back an olive branch in her bill, next time she went out, she did not come back, so Noah knew it be safe to come out. Earth all anew, was now up to Noah and his family to start filling the earth up with folks again, so de had lots of chillum, grand chillum and so on.

Section III

Prayers Must be Taught

Whenever it was time for us to go to bed for the night, as always we had to pray before we went to sleep. Everyone prayed, including my Pa Willie and my Mama Willie Mae.

Grandma Anna taught us to say:

> Lawd, as I lay me down to sleep
> I pray de Lawd my soul to keep
> If I should die before I wake up
> I pray de Lawd my soul to take
> If I should live another day
> I pray de Lawd to guide my way.
> Amen

Then she would say: "good night chillum" and would kiss each one of us in the middle of our forehead, even our Mama and Papa. We would hug her neck and say "Good night Grandma Anna."

Grandma Anna and the Mole

One morning I awaken to hear all this chopping and talking outside. I got dressed and went outside foe we left for the bacca fields. Grandpa Job was seated on his favorite stump, quietly watching his wife, my Grandma Anna, chop, chop, chop at some mounds of dirt in the yard. I asked him "Grandpa Job what is she doing?" "Just have a seat and watch."

So I took his advice. For several days we had noticed raised mounds of dirt in the yard. Grandma Anna never said anything, but every day she examined that mound of dirt. What she did this morning before daybreak, was to stick a pitch fork about five feet above the end of the tunnel, and then stuck another pitchfork at the end of the mound. When the morning came she set out to chop, chop, chopping, just as fast as she could, pulling that dirt from the mound, still talking to herself rather than us. She would stop for a while and listen, wipe some sweat away with her apron, then began chop, chop, chopping away again.

That pitch folk was moving so fast, your eyes go up, down, up again, just trying to follow its movements.

Sweat pouring down Grandma Anna's face, running down from under her head wrap scarf. Still talking to herself, "nothing but trouble", "just gonna cause pain," not if I can help it you won't!"

Wham! Out pops a black ball of fur. I jumped to my feet and ran over to get a better look, looked just like a furry ball to me, his fur was beautiful and very soft almost like the wild otters you would see from time to time swimming in the creek. Grandma Anna told us to touch the fur, but be careful, she thought he was died, but not sure. We did touch it lightly, you could not see its eyes or ears, they were covered with fur, but those claws! They were the longest claws I'd ever seen on any animal, they were well suited for digging under the ground. Grubs and earthworms did not stand a chance against those claws!

With the mole lying there, small and still, Grandma Anna leaned on the hoe she had been chopping with and said "Now!" "Now what?" I asked, she answered, "now your Grandpa Job can walk safely in this yard without tripping in a mole mound tunnel."

"You see Lucy Mae, your Grandpa Job walks cripple, if he stepped on a mole mound tunnel the dirt would give way and down he would go, maybe breaking something again. He to old now to have bones breaking on him. You see I cannot run the risk of that happening to him, therefore the mole had to be dealt with."

My brother Ruben had gotten up by then and came outside. Seeing that little old dead mole was right down his alley. He said, "Gotta have a funeral for this poor little old mole," Runt (JW), our baby brother in the family went "yuck!"

Nobody bothered to volunteer to help or attend this silly gathering, so Ruben had the funeral for, as he named him, "Wrong-way Mole." Years late, no one in the family was surprised that he became a Pastor for a large church in Atlanta, Georgia. He always wanted to preach and conduct funerals.

Learned lessons about how life works we saw every day of our lives. Grandma Anna always said: "we should always consider what is best for all, concerning any incident that arises in your life. Sometimes you have to be the one who says what has to be done, maybe hard, she would say, "but it is fair." I listened to what she said always, and I remembered it all down through the years, what a great teacher she was! She had God given "Common Sense."

Love and the Hoot Owl

"Love is de greatest gift of all Lucy Mae". "God himself is love, and He gave for us, you and me, a son who gave His life to save us. What greater love can you ask for than just to be loved in such a way? Just as I love you Baby Girl?"

She gave me a great big hug and always that tender familiar sweet kiss right in the middle of my forehead.

"Lucy Mae I cannot not read and write Baby Girl, slaves not allowed to learn, against the law, just as it is for you and your brothers right now, but there will come a day when everything will change and you will learn everything, but in the meantime look and learn by seeing and listening, the more you listen the more you learn." "Always remember that one of these days you and your brothers will learn to read and write."

"You know that old hoot owl that sets in that tree outside and hoots?"

"Yes ma'am."

"You and your brothers be like that old hoot owl that sets in that tree. Got those big round eyes that can see in the dark, them funny little tuffs of feathers that look like ears sticking up? Can hear a mouse running across the ground, swoops down, silently. That mouse becomes dinner or supper." We both laughed.

"Some folks say that old hoot owl can turn his head all the way around" Baby Girl that not true. "He turns his head half way around just like we do. Never miss seeing a thing though. Turn his head halfway around to listen better. Best we should follow his methods."

"One of these days Lucy Mae, you will learn how to read and write, speak correctly, meet other people from different places, and be able to hold your own with them. Grandma Anna will be long gone by then, but I will see you as a grown woman, and your brothers as grown men, and I will be so proud of all of you, what a long way you will go. You will always have the joy of remembering the talks that you and I have." I said "Grandma Anna, you like that old hoot owl, the wisest woman I know."

Grandma Anna said "Whooo me?" Grandma Anna was so funny at times!

Growing up and becoming the educated woman my Grandma Anna wanted me to be was always my prayer to God. Oh God, please Lord, let it happen!

Her words of knowledge, skills and determinations spring now from the very depths of my soul as I advanced in age and remember her.

Oh, Grandma Anna, remembering you brings a smile to my face and tears to my eyes. Her saying was "be as wise as an owl and as gentle as a dove."

Research Project: There are many species of owls in the world. Research these and list some facts about each.

Have you ever seen a live owl?

Can you describe what he looked like?

Look up the following owls listed below and write something about them.

Which owl would be your favorite?

1.   Great Gray

2.   Snowy owl

3.   Eagle owl

4.   Barn owl

5.   Barred owl

6.   Burring owls

Fun activity: Try your skill on drawing an owl.

Snake Bite

Summertime brings so many good foods you can eat and enjoy just by picking them right off the trees or vines. Apples, peaches, pears and plums, grapes, and many others.

The plum trees had blossomed and you could tell just by the number of bees hanging around the blossoms that these plums would be the best ever, sweet as sugar! Jams and jellies would be made from them and preserved for the long winter months to enjoy with biscuits or even kusk.

Grandma Anna had warned us about going into the plum orchard or any locations where other fruit bearing trees or vines were growing without an adult being with us, including the blackberry patches. She said snakes loved fruit and could always be found around the places they grew, and then too, it was a good hunting ground for snakes to catch small animals and birds that were fruit eaters that visited the places where the fruit had fallen to the ground, plus she said "snakes could climb the trees to reach the non-fallen fruit".

One day my brothers and I decided we would go pick some plums, eat them there in the plum orchard and no one would know what we had done, so away we went, the four of us, JW, Andrew, Ruben and myself and our bare feet!

Life on the ground around the plum trees was a busy place, teeming with ants, bees, insects, squirrels and birds, who flew away when we approached. We were so excited. My brothers begin chasing each other in the open spaces around the plum trees.

JW was running and turning cart wheels, one right after the other.

The soft warm grass felt soothing as I ran my toes through it. Several spots in the orchard had bear spots where no grass was growing, just dirt. I dung my toes deeply into the ground. Making marks that I never knew one day would become words and having meanings.

Raising both my arms in the air, I begin turning in circles, feeling the wind blowing against my raised arms. Stopping suddenly and catching my balance, I stood looking at the blue sky, big fluffy clouds drifting, they looked like cotton balls. Yesterday I had seen that same sky while working the bacca field, but it was a beautiful blue, cloudless.

Shifting my attention away from the sky, I headed for the tree where my brothers were. They were busy using sticks trying to knock down the good ones they could not reach.

We did not want the ones that had fallen to the ground, in most cases they had become bruised and half eaten by something, therefore we focused on picking special ones from the tree.

Laughing, playing, and enjoying eating fresh ripe sweet plums, we were really having fun, when all of a sudden we hear this screaming coming from Andrew. We stopped eating and ran to him. Slithering away in the grass from Andrew was this big snake. Poor Andrew was still screaming, crying and holding his foot. I yelled "Ruben go and get Aunt Sadie, tell her what happened and to come help." Off Ruben shot like a bullet heading toward Aunt Sadie's cabin which was close to the plum orchard. Aunt Sadie heard him yelling, calling her name before he got to the cabin. Aunt Sadie, holding her long dress up, came running toward us. Ruben pointed toward the plum tree. When she reached the tree, Andrew still screaming was sitting there cuddling that foot and screaming for dear life.

Aunt Sadie picked him up and started running toward her cabin. When we got there, she placed Andrew on the bed, told us to hold him down. That boy was howling, twisting, turning, jumping and Aunt Sadie yelling "Hold him still, hold him still you two!" We were doing the best we could to hold him down. She got a sharp knife from off the kitchen table, held his foot up toward her chest and cut an "X" in the exact place where the snake had bitten him, and then squeezed hard, squeezing and pressing all that poison from his foot.

That boy was screaming and howling like nobody's business. Aunt Sadie put some kerosene on that snake bite, rubbing it into the "X" she had cut on his foot.

She wrapped that foot up with some old cloth she had.

This did not stop his crying, but at least the yelling had died down. Aunt Sadie told me to go and tell Grandma Anna what had happened. I headed for our cabin. Getting there I told Grandma Anna what had happened, she never said a word, except, "Let's go." Off we headed marching toward to Aunt Sadie's cabin.

When we got to the cabin Grandma Anna and I went in, there on the bed lay poor Andrew, still hurting and looking real pitiful. The first thing he said was "Grandma Anna I'm sorry, you told us not to go there without a grown person with us, we didn't mind you, and I know that." "I'm sorry".

Grandma Anna looked at all of us and said two words, "Lesson Learned." And that was that, she never mentioned it again. Taking Andrew in her arms, throwing him over her shoulder like a sack of feed, we headed for home. Nobody saying a word, just feet slapping the ground as we walked. My stomach hurt! Did not know what was to happen when we reached home.

Grandpa Job did not say a word when he saw us, just shook his head.

Speaking of snakes again, I know someone who hated snakes worse than my snake bitten brother, my Grandpa Job! He did not like snakes at all, if he saw one before the snake saw him and slithered away, that snake was a died snake.

We had a type of shed or "lean to" in the back of the cabin where we kept our one cow. One morning Grandpa Job went to milk that old cow, he said he noticed that cow looked like she was in a trance, just standing there.

He looked down just as he placed the bucket to set on, on the ground while he milked the cow, right there under the cows utter was a snake that had raised himself up to so he could reach the cows "tit", had his mouth on it just sucking milk to beat the band! Grandpa got up, moved the bucket back and set the one he was going to catch the milk in further back. Took that old tree limb walking stick he used, aimed, swung, knocked that snake one way, the trance cow jumped another! When that snake landed further out in the yard, you could hear Grandpa Job yelling, 'yes ma'am, yes ma'am! One down dead, fifty to a hundred more to go!"

By that time all of us had come out of the cabin to stand and look and laugh.

That man did not like snakes! Well you know who shows up, here comes the "funeral man," my brother, for a snake funeral and burial. I guess he handled it himself. Everybody went back to what they were doing at first getting ready for another day of hard work.

Grandpa Job took some lye soap and water and washed the utters of that cow, the milk he drew from them he threw away, said we did not need to drink any milk behind and old "milk snake." Years later I have heard similar stories about "Milk Snakes" drinking milk from cows.

Aunt Grace

How do I describe Aunt Grace? She was Aunt Sadie sister. Aunt Grace was the main cook at the big house. If it could be eaten, Aunt Grace could cook it. And she could hold her ground too. There might be something or someone Aunt Grace was scared of, but we have never seen it or them. A medium height women, with her share of meat on her big frame, which gave her the appearance of "I don't take no stuff off nobody."

Aunt Grace had a terrible looking scar on her face that ran from her temple to her chin on the right side of her face. This scar was from the hands of her first owner's overseer. Grandma Anna said "at first it looked like it had took half her face away", but when it finally healed was not as bad as it had looked at first. They kept a poultice of sulfur, sugar and grease on her face, this cure had to be worn every day for more than six months Grandma Anna say. After that, Aunt Grace's owner asked Masa Mathis to take Aunt Grace to his plantation, "pay me $50.00 dollars and she's yours" he said, and that's how she got over here with us. Feelings of hate between that Overseer and Aunt Grace was gonna lead to some one getting killed, more than likely Aunt Grace, not the overseer. Seems this bad treatment of Aunt Grace made her the tough woman she is now. Aunt Grace would say," you treat a person like a dog, don't be surprised if and when that dog turns and bites you, a hit dog will holler, and given the time he will learn to hate you. That's when the feelings sticks forever." As she would say, "like white on rice."

Grandma Anna, Aunt Sadie and Aunt Grace were the strong, brave, older women the younger plantation females slaves looked up to. Wise women! Wise beyond their years! Having weathered a lot of storms in their lives, and when they speak they speak with the voices of experience.

Aunt Grace helped Grandma Anna with the birthing of all the babies that are born in Bethel.

Those Old Turkeys

That old Tom Turkey bird, just strutting around in those woods, making all that noise, saying to the them hens, "Here I am, look at me, come see me, see how my feathers shine in the sun!"

"When I spread my tail feathers and drag my wing on the ground, don't I just look like the most handsome Tom you lady turkeys have ever seen?"

Grandma Anna said "all that fussing and strutting he was doing said to the other Tom turkeys" don't you come over here, all this is my territory and these my hens."

But she said "what that old Tom Turkey needed to be worried about was becoming some body's Thanksgiving Dinner" in the "Big House" and in the slave cabins.

She said Indians hunted him with bow and arrow, but folks in Tennessee used the "bang" "bang" stick, that be called the rifle. Slaves were not allowed to use fire arms, therefore the turkeys they got had to be killed and given to them.

If November weather in Tennessee was fairly mild, in which most cases it was, turkeys were dipped in hot water that was boiling in the outside kettle. Preparing a turkey was not an easy job, that water in the kettle had to be boiling, if not those feathers stuck like glue to that old bird, so water was always boiling hot.

Grandma Anna was an expert on plucking turkey feathers, that Tom or Hen was just plain naked when she finished the plucking. The neck and feet were removed, next the innards were removed.

Grandma Anna with her hand would go inside that turkey bird, make one strong pull and out came everything. Liver and gizzards were set aside for use later in the dressing and gravies the cooks made, or for making turkey foot soup.

Turkey feet toe nails was cut off. The feet were skinned and boiled down. Making a broth that could be used for seasoning or drinking. Flavor with salt and pepper, turkey foot soup also tasted good with fried kusk (A receipt that came with my ancestors from Africa). Kusk is corn meal and hot boiling water plus red pepper, with a pinch of sugar mixed in, rolled into a ball, and dropped in hot grease, fried, and eaten. Grandpa Job would mix his kusk up in his hot turkey foot soup. He loved it. I was not too sold on it, but it did warm you up inside. I smile to myself remembering those nights with my family long ago eating turkey foot soup and kusk.

Turkey foot soup was used to ward off colds or "chill blains" as the old folks used to call colds and fevers. Real sick, old folks with stomach problems, would suck the tender little yellow pieces of flesh between the bones in the feet. Them little pieces of meat tasted good to them, and it did not hurt they stomach either.

If kept sitting by the hearth to keep it warm, turkey foot soup made a good drink of something hot before you went to bed in those drafty cabins. Our cabin was not flat on the ground like many cabins were, it was built up with a wooden floor in it. It was still drafty though and sleeping on the floor your bones socked in the coldness every night.

For the families that did not have Turkey for eating, there was always the old "Possum Pot Dinner" for Thanksgiving or Christmas.

Kill, skin, and clean that possum like you would any other animal. Put old Mr. Opossum in a boiling pot, hang on the big hook over the fire in the fireplace, and let him cook down, peel some sweet potatoes and onions, put in the same pot with him and then just wait.

That smell was so good, tasted good too, but Lawd! The grease he had in him, like lard! No wonder he waddle around so fat.

Then there is always raccoon known as "coon." Coon did not see a boiling pot, no sir! His place was the frying pan. Grandma Anna could fry coon so pretty and brown, folks thought it was fried chicken.

Mr. Samuel and his son Phillip would stop by from time to time, they were either coming from the baca fields or going to the baca fields to work. Other times they were going or coming from fishing and gigging for turtles.

They always manage to bring Grandma Anna a mud catfish or either a turtle. This day when they came by and set a spell, Grandma Anna had fried a coon. Phillip always said he did not like coon, so at dinners that was held after church sometimes, he would avoid the fried coon platter like that old raccoon gonna jump up off that plate and wear him out with them sharp claws on those little old hands and feet!

They are mean little critters too!

Mr. Samuel said to Grandma Anna, "Anna, been killing and frying chickens today?" "Yes I have Samuel, you and Phillip help yourself to some, gotta enough to share," well they dived in. Mr. Samuel knew what it was. He and Grandma Anna winked at each other. They both looked at me, I covered the smile on my face with my hands.

It was the week end and Pastor Pappy Merry arrived to preach his monthly sermon. When Pastor Merry first came to Bethel Masa John had told Grandpa Job that Pastor Merry was to stay with us, and that was that, no questions asked. Grandpa Job said "alright Sir" as if he could have said anything else but "alright Sir."

Grandpa Job told Pastor to put his grip inside the cabin, then come outside to join us. Grandma Anna told him to get him a plate and help himself. He did. Pastor Merry had eaten coon before so he knew what it was too.

"Phillip, how your piece of chicken taste?" Mr. Samuel asked "Good Papa, how about yours?"

"Tis lip smacking good son, Miss Anna is one good cook." "Yes Sir" Phillip said while he was eating. When they got ready to leave to head home Grandma Anna asked Phillip if he wanted some fried coon to carry home to eat.

"No ma'am thank you Miss Anna, can't stand that stuff, rather have fried chicken like you just had any day I can get it before I eat some old bad tasting "coon." Pappy Merry, Grandma, Mr. Samuel and me bent over laughing!

"What? yall laughing about?" Phillip asked.

Grandma Anna picked up the platter held it toward Phillip and said to Phillip would you like some more "coon" Phillip? Phillip looked sick, but he held that coon down, did not puke it up.

Welcome to the world of "coon" Phillip, Pastor Merry said.

Phillip just stood there.

Moral of this story: Don't knock it until you have tried it!

Many folks have ate "coon" and smacked their lips over that "good fried chicken." Grandma Anna and I would look at each other, I would whisper to her "coons and chickens, folks don't know no difference!" she laughed. She knew exactly who I was talking about, Phillip! And those other folks eating and smacking never knowing it be coon meat either.

Squirrels

Squirrels had to be given to us by someone that had gone hunting. Slaves and ex-slaves were not allowed to own guns or rifles as I said before. Overseers that hunted squirrels would give them away to anyone who wanted them. They hunted them for sport, not for eating.

Sometimes when my brothers and I would be walking from the fields in the fall of the year after all the leaves had fallen from the trees, we would see this bunch of dried leaves like a ball in the notches of tree limbs.

We asked Grandpa Job what they were. He said they were squirrels nest. Hunters would just "boom", shoot right into that nest, and the squirrels would come tumbling down. Hunters would just go and pick them up. Better make sure they are good and dead when you pick them up though, the little bogeys are tough, and they will bite the heck out of you! One thing I learned about squirrels, one little old squirrel can make more racket that four or five deer walking and grazing, he can flatten himself on the ground as flat as a pancake, Grandma Anna say "he be spreading his scent into what he think his territory." Squirrels would starve to death in the winter if'n they did not prepare for the long cold spell they had to face. Grandma Anna said," that's how God cares for us. He lets us work and save for the future, and He meets our needs when things are scarce (Prov.12:11). God gives us seasons of plenty so we can live when things are not plentiful (Psalm 23).

Squirrels could be skinned and cleaned, then baked, boiled or fried. Grandma Anna said she had an Uncle that would fry the squirrel brain and eat it, I asked her, why? She said, he said it was good for your eyesight. I asked her did it help him, she laughed and said "might have helped, might not have helped, but it did not harm him!" that statement bought a smile to both our faces.

Grandpa Job had this old blue tick hound dog he named "Bottom." That old dog was good for nothing, I mean nothing. Would not even bark when someone coming toward the cabin, and too lazy to even twitch his ear to flick a fly off. Our cabin had a floor in it and was built up high, so his favorite place was under the cabin in a dust hole he had dug to keep himself cool in the summer, and warm in the winter, since the chimney went to the ground under the cabin, he slept against the chimney, unless it got to cold, then he would head to the lean to and sleep in there with the cow.

One day he comes trotting around the cabin, with a squirrel in his mouth, it was dead as a doorknob. He dropped it at Grandpa Job's feet, as if to say" here's my keep, don't say I never helped to bring in food to this family." Grandpa Job threw it across the road. That crazy old dog, ears flopping in the air, tongue hanging out and juice flying from his mouth, went looping across the road, brought it back and dropped him at Grandpa Job's feet again. This time Grandpa Job threw the squirrel up in a tree, it did not fall down, got caught on a limb and stayed there.

That dumb old hound dog sat there the rest of the day and night watching and waiting for that squirrel to fall. It didn't. Grandpa said he had never seen a hound dog pointing sitting, supposed to be standing with his tail pointed straight out! Not Bottom, he too lazy for that.

My brothers learned how to make bird traps. Birds were trapped, cleaned, gutted and stuck on a piece of wood to be roasted over the fire in the hearth for eating. Snow birds were the easiest. Those would be the doves, robins and black birds. Inside the box used for trapping my brothers would use pieces of food stuck on bushes, when the birds would get close one small stick holding the box up would collapse, all the boys had to do was to take them out and avoid getting pecked, snap their necks and they were ready for cleaning. Many slave families enjoyed meals that were roasted "snow birds".

Nancy L. B. Vaughan

I asked Grandma Anna why they were called "snow birds" when they were robin red breast, doves and black birds. She said folks say they always bring the snows with them when they come. When folks would see these birds they would always say "big snow storm coming."

These are some of the Thanksgiving foods we ate.

Moral of this story: Make the best of what you have and be thankful for that, cause things could be worse.

Rabbits

What can you say about rabbits? Lawd they some good eating if the cook who is cooking them know how to cook them. Grandma Anna show knows how to cook rabbits, frying them, making gravy and biscuits. Only thing is, you can only eat rabbits in the late fall and winter. Summertime they have worms in them called "wolves" which were tapeworms they picked up through they feet from the ground and animal droppings, to nasty to eat in Spring and Summer, but Grandma Anna say "the Lawd had his reasons for doing that too," seems to me she would say like God say, "if we eat them all the time, what time would they have to have babies and rebuild up they numbers?" My Grandma Anna had good reasoning.

There be another season at the plantation. This be "Hog killing season." Some folks call it "Hog killing time," either way it be time for Masa John to decide how many and which hogs he gonna kill. He usually likes to get the killings done before the Christmas holidays arrive. If a cold snap did not get here in December, then killing time would have to move on down to February, and nobody likes that, just to cold.

Everybody at Cedar Grove help with hog killing, even Grandpa Job. Sometimes Masa John have to hire other plantation owners and they slaves to help if'n, say a hundred hogs were killed, or even fifty.

Hog killing morning be cold as kraut. Masa John and all the men walk down to the hog pens there on the plantation.

No black men allowed to handle a shot gun or rifle, so they would cut the ones to be killed out from the others who not being killed. Masa John fire the rifle straight into the head of each hog. Those helping to drag the dead ones out be dragging them to the side, so they all be carried to the cleaning place at one time.

The men hang the hogs up on thick wires that had heavy metal hooks hanging on them that run from one tree to another. The back legs of the hogs has tough pieces of meat that when the hogs was hanging would support his weight. Cleaning areas were located close to the cleaning tables where they would butcher the hogs.

Wash pots of boiling water be bubbling, causing steam when it hit the cold air. The fire crackling and blazing up around and under the pot, I could not tell the smoke coming from the fires from the vapor we be breathing in and out our nose and mouth it's so cold. Inside of the pots of boiling water are heavy blankets of cloths.

The men lifted these cloths out with heavy sticks, placing them over the hogs. This was done several times to soften the hair on the hog so it can be scraped off. There were four men working on each hog. My papa, Uncle Big Bud, Luke and Mr. Limb. As soon as they finish one, they start on another one.

Scraping carefully so the fat under the skin would not be damaged cause this skin would be boiled down for making lard. While the other two held the hog steady Uncle Big Bud took one of the cane cutting knives and sliced the hog straight down the middle from his hind legs to the throat part. Papa had told me to put a tub under the hog to catch the inners as they fell out. I did, and they came dropping down causing steam in the coldness. The tub of inners went into the hand of the women, me included, where the parts are separated and cleaned. Cooking pots were going cause some of the inners, such as livers and lites, were cooked and canned in jars that day to be used from the long winter months into the spring months.

The skin was removed and the women took it to start melting it down into lard, the pieces of skin became brown and crispy, these were called "cracklings." Everybody eat dem cracklings, and they mix them in the kusk when they cook it. The cooking had to be done right, let the skin cook to long the lard be yellow and smell hoggish. The fat around the kidneys make the best pure white lard for cake making and pie pastry, everybody let Aunt Grace do this rending, she was the best in cooking that kind of special lard down.

Folks that were working with the hog killing had to be feed, so neckbones, backbones, and none special parts of the meat was were being cooked, to be served with fried kusk with cracklings mixed in it and black eyed peas for those working with the killing.

Dogs, even Bottom had a heyday, lapping up any and everything they could get cooked and uncooked, didn't make no difference.

Bladders were special. They were saved, blown up, hung and left to dry. When they were dried dem hog bladders were balls for the chillums to play wit.

The intestines were put in a wheel barrel and rolled down to the creek where they held them, dipping them up and down in the water til all of what was inside floated on the water and slowly sank to the bottom of the creek. Then they brought them back to us women folk and we finished the cleaning. Dese things called "chitlings". You talk about smelling!

The best parts of the hog, the hams, shoulders, bacon, sowbelly, and tender loins was for Masa John and he family. Sausage had to be ground up and seasoned, den stuffed into cloth sacks. Ribs could not be cured, so ribs, feet, ears, tails and brains, and any other left overs were given to slaves and overseers that helped with the killing. Luke's (my Mama's brother) special was tending the hogsheads. Masa John always kept enough of the pig ears to make sure he had enough for hogshead cheese. He loved him some hogshead cheese. Luke and some of the other men did the boiling of the heads down to make hogshead cheese or souse. Masa John say "Luke make the best souse in Rutherford county." Luke got another job on the plantation too. Some where he learned how to play a fiddle. Masa John be smiling and grinning all the time when he speak of Luke and his fiddling. Masa John be the only plantation owner that have a slave to play for parties. Luke got special clothes . . . a suit, shirt, necktie, and shiny shoes, so all he did would stand and play for hours for weddings, Christmas and all other holidays and special events.

All the special parts of the meat had to be cured for as long as a year, the longer it be cured, the better it taste. Meat was hung in a smoke house where hickory or cedar wood was slowly burned to make the smoke, that smoke help in the curing.

Grandma Anna say in curing meat you better get the saltpeter, black pepper, red pepper, sugar and spices mixture rubbed in every part of the meat or it draw flies, dem flies lay eggs on the meat and "blow it" and "skippers"(worms) get inside. So folk that were curers were very careful and thickly covered every inch of that meat. Folks that had meat that had spoiled still did not throw the spoiled meat away though, when they boiled something wit the meat those worms just float to the top of the water and they just skim the worms of the top of the water as they float to the top and throw them away. Dogs want even eat them! Dey maggots!

Section IV

Joe Quack

When you had pets they were usually animals that was a part of the plantation, not nothing you could really call your own special "pal" and "pet." Grandpa Job had these ducks. They hatched baby ducks, all nice furry and yellow. One little tiny one seemed to take a shine to me, and me to him. Oh, by the way he was a "him." Grandpa Job told me I could have him if I promised to take care of him. I was so happy, something that was finally mind! I named him "Joe Quack", if I had pockets on what I was wearing, Joe went into my pockets, getting a free ride from place to place, with his head peeking over the top of the pocket. My own special pet, nobody else's "Joe Quack." Joe never stayed in the house at night, he slept under the cabin with Grandpa Job's old hound dog. Even before 1860 folks were still running away from evil overseers, and when traveling they need shelter, clothing and food. Joe Quack disappeared one day, the same time some runaways came through our area. Guess he became some-body's dinner and source of food. Do I miss my duck? Yes, I do!, but Grandma Anna told me to live and let live, that someone needed that duck for food, if they had not needed him they would not have taken him. I never had another pet again, hurts too bad to lose a pet or a relative as well, no need to experience that heart ache again. Once in a lifetime is enough.

Moral of this story: Once is for always in losses, no need to go for seconds, but seconds come on their own. That's a given!

Games

How do you play games that you have never seen? Such was the case with slave children. The children made games of everyday actions they saw taking place in their lives. Trapping, fishing, playing marbles, ball, chasing and wading in the creeks.

Some games were the exact actions they had observed in their lives, one example of this was "whippings" that were given to runaway slaves, slaves that were considered "trouble makers" by being disobedient, stealing, talking back, lying, or just refusing to look down when speaking, or being spoken to. These were some of the actions that would bring on beatings for a slave.

Sad part of this be, white overseer would use the strongest slave on the plantation to do the whipping, whipping his own kind, but if he not obey dese rules, he might be hung or shot. Doomed if you did and doomed if'n you don't.

Whippings, running, dodging, pretend crying, and jumping up and down would be the way the children who had seen someone get a whipping would act, that would be the way they played out the scenes. Grandma Anna would never let us play that game, she would just tell us, "you will understand it better by and by."

My brother Ruben would always like to have funerals. I did not care for this type of playing, so I set them out, leaving him to have Andrew and JW trapped into hearing him. Poor JW would be bored stiff, but too scared to complain.

Grandma Anna, when she had the time, would make us "spin buttons."

Spin buttons were strings threaded through buttons and tied. We could spin these buttons with our hands in all directions.

Slave children never had any new toys, maybe a cast off once in a while from one of Masa Mathis Grand children. Misses Sarah would give them to Mama and Joyce (Joyce is my Mama's sister-in-law, she married to my Mama's brother Luke) to pass on to us.

When fall would come and the corn in the fields was drying up, Grandma Anna would make me "corn cob dolls." The shucks still had to be on the ear of corn, she would twist the shucks this way and that way, tying them together, before you know it she had made a doll. For the eyes and nose she would mark with charcoal, for the lips, the red stains from any berry she found, if no berries, then no lips were put on her, but she was still special, with or without lips, because my Grandma Anna had loved me enough to create a special doll for me.

Now when we went to church on Sundays I had a doll to carry with me, just like the little white girls had. Their dolls were cloth handkerchief dolls that they Mamas made them for them. They were called "silent dolls" because when they were accidently dropped on the floor they did not make any noise. Didn't have to worry about my doll making noise on dropping her, I was not going to drop her, she was too special!

Somewhere back in African, children learned the art of playing with marbles. They may have been carved from gems in the Motherland of Africa. Grandpa Job made some for my brothers to play with out of red clay dirt. Those would sometimes wear out and break. To replace those broken ones and adds new ones that would last, he carved tiny round wooden balls for them to play with. African children learn to play "pick-up-sticks", we played that game too, "one two buckle my shoe, three four close the door, five six pick up dem sticks."

My brothers loved to chase. Small animals, chickens, each other, just anything that would run, even in the bacca fields they would chase me with those bacca worms. They knew I was scared of them, and they knew I would run. One day I just got tired of running, stopped and stood my ground, ready for a fight! My Daddy, Willie, clapped his hands. He was so proud of his only girl standing up for herself. Shocked my brothers too!

That I was really going to fight them. No more throwing bacca worms, at least not at me!

Jumping rope was another game we played, at least my cousin Rachael and I did.

Rachael was my mother's brother's (Luke's) daughter. Joyce was Rachael's Mama. They too lived on plantation "Cedar Grove". We would spend days and nights at each of our parent's cabins. Having no sister, Rachael was almost like my sister. Jumping rope was our favorite game. My brothers said, "jumping rope was for girls, not boys." We liked that, it got them out of our way!

There were plenty of trees growing around us. Some of these trees were "old sage orange trees." Folks said "horses ate the round green fruit that grew on them, so many folks called them "horse oranges," I never seem no horse or much of anything else eating them.

My brothers, Rachael, her sisters and brothers and myself would play something call "Annie Over." We would use old sage oranges for balls.

Some of us would get in front of the cabin and the others in the back, someone would yell, "Annie over, here she comes," and the others side would answer "let her roll!" We played this game for hours, but one thing about them old sage oranges they let off sticky white juice, that juice would dry on our hands and we had fun peeling the dried juice scales off our hands, to see whose piece would come off the biggest without tearing up.

Oh yes, forgot to tell you, I finally saw a squirrel eating the seeds from these oranges! Guess they were good for something.

Sometimes Grandma had enough scraps of clothe to tear them in strips, gradually winding them together into a ball. When she finished my brothers were the happiest folk in the world, they spent hours tossing that ball, running and hitting it with sticks. As an adult remembering their playing, I see the same movement in some games played today.

Grandpa Job loved carving wooden things, especially bowls for Grandma Anna, her favorite was the biscuit bowl for kneading dough in. He made toys for my brothers. He would make little spinning tops for my brothers and Rachael's little brothers. They spent hours of the spare time they had seeing who's top could spin the longest.

Research: The Old Sage Tree: Draw a picture of an old sage orange. Ask your parents to show you a live old sage orange tree if there are any growing where you live.

Christmas Coming

Holiday Season getting here pretty soon, hurry, hurry, hurry, can't wait. Two weeks before Christmas we begin to worry Grandma Anna to start telling the Christmas story about the birth of Jesus. These are the stories preacher man had preached down through the years and Grandma Anna knew it all by heart, which meant she remembered all she ever hear about it. I have so much to tell about getting ready for the holidays, I'll get back to Grandma Anna's stories later.

December come Masa John and Misses Sarah start getting the house ready for Christmas. Sometimes visitors would come for Christmas. Depending on the weather in Tennessee they might get snowed in for a while, but that did not seem to matter to anyone, just made the vacation Holiday fun last longer. Folks would just wait for a "spring thaw" which sometimes came in January or early February, where the weather is almost like spring time and the snow would melt. More snow would fall later, but that warm melting time was called the "spring thaw." Never heard anyone complaining about having visitors too long.

Visitors would stay until there was a "winter thaw", which meant the weather would clear-up enough for the roads to become passable for travel.

Everybody that worked in the big house rushing around, cleaning, painting, cooking, just in general sprucing up everywhere.

Misses Sarah told Mama to bring me and Rachael to the big house to get us started on learning how to be house servants. Every morning we headed for the big house, Rachael would come to work from her own cabin with her Mama Joyce.

Grandpa Job was already at the big house firing up the hearths and stoves. When you walk into the kitchen, it smells go good. Cinnamon, allspice, nutmeg, vanilla, all kinds of good holiday smells. Once the outside and the inside of the house were decorated with cedar wreathes and Christmas trees, they just added to the good smells.

Masa John would take my brothers and Rachael's brothers out to gather cedar trees to use in decorations and for Christmas trees in different parts of the "big house." In addition to gathering cedar trees, they picked every bush that had red berries or white berries on them. Those with the white berries were called "mistletoe"; they had to climb the trees to get those. White folks say "if someone was standing under the mistletoe, "They would be kissed." White folks stuff, not for colors Missus Mathis say. Didn't make no difference to me know how, didn't want nobody kissing on me except my Grandma Anna.

Masa John would tie all the cedars collected together and the boys would bring them on their shoulders back to the house. Misses Sarah would tell Mama, Grace or one of the other cooks to give them a treat, which to me seemed like such a small reward. Have you ever handled a cedar tree and in cold weather too? Stickers and needles went right into your hands! Don't guess my brothers and cousins cared . . . they were too busy enjoying the home made fudge candies.

Fruit loafs, sweet potato pies, cinnamon breads, butter rolls, lady fingers, all kinds of candies, country ham cooking, all this for Christmas celebration, and them turkeys.

Black walnuts and Hickory nuts that had been gathered in the fall of the year were now ready to be cracked and get the nuts inside them out. Cooks in the big house used this time as a time for resting and talking among themselves while some cracked the nuts open and others picked them out. Anything that hit the floor was picked up and used, no wasting goodies here!

We had a black walnut tree in our front yard at the cabin. When black walnuts fell from the tree, Grandma told us not to touch them after they turned black, because the juice that came out would stain our fingers "black."

Nancy L. B. Vaughan

To bust the outer hull away Grand mama would do this:

Take a big stick and beat the hull loose. She told us to leave the walnut alone until it dried on its own, and then we would gather them up and carry them inside, before the squirrels begin carrying them away.

The meat inside the walnut had the best taste ever in cakes, pies, candies and cookies, or for just plain eating.

These little hickory nuts were hard to get anything out of they, they were so tiny, Mama said "they probably gave the squirrels a headache trying to open them too" all the women laughed. Rachael's Mama, Joyce said, "Amen!"

There was a big open hearth in the kitchen . . . the cooks would bury sweet potatoes in the ashes for roasting. They would smell so good when they start cooking, the skins would get kind of crispy and could be eaten and the juice in them sweet taters was sweet just like sugar.

These treats were given to the children and of course Grandpa Job was given enough for him and Grandma Anna to eat, plus they kept his hands warm while he was walking back to our cabin. Wrap them in some cloth, putting them in his pocket, did two things, they stayed hot and warmed his hands which he stuck into his coat pocket.

Before the cold weather set in the Masa John would call all the slaves to the big house and have the women that sewed measure everyone for new winter clothes. These items were given at Christmas time. Clothes fitting for summer was carried out the same way, these summer clothes were given out at Easter. Each slave was given two pair of pants for the men and boys, one pair metal toed shoes, two shirts, and two outer coats, socks and a shawl. Women were given two blouses, two skirts, several aprons, shawls, a coat and shoes. If the outfits were being made for house servants the quality of the material used was a better texture and pattern. Why? I asked Mama, she said, "house servants had interactions with the plantation family daily, also guest they may have, therefore they wanted them dressed properly."

Missus Sarah would tell everyone "cleanness was next to godlessness." What that meant, I don't know, just one more of her sayings. Sometimes Rachael and me thought she was crazy! Later as I learn more I came to understand about that saying of hers. God loved cleanness too, that why he made laws for his chosen people on what they could eat and drink so they would not get sick. After learning that the saying did not seem so odd to me.

Beginning of Educated

The year was 1856. Rachael and me had turned sixteen years old. My cousin Rachael, oh beautiful Rachael! Folks that not 'spose to be looking at her looked!, when Rachael came into view all eyes were on her. She looked like an angel. Skin like satin, big brown eyes with long lashes. Her hair was naturally curly, but you could not see it, cause she be wearing a head rags like all the other slave women wear. Me and her bout the same height now, but you can look at Rachael and tell she gonna be tall like her Mama Joyce. Grandma Anna said Rachael and her Mama Joyce be what colors call "mulatto". She say they went back and took looks from Joyce's Grand pappy. I ask her "how?" she said that be a long time ago and no need to talk about that now, not gonna change a thing. I could see that it was bothering her when I kept asking questions, so I hushed. The only thing she would always say was "Joyce and Luke had some nice looking chillum."

Sometime when Rachael and me be working around the big house we could see Misses Sarah watching us. We don't know why.

Misses Sarah called us into the sitting room or as they sometimes called it "Masa John's study." She started doing this every day after Rachael and me had finished our tasks around the big house.

This was the beginning of our book learning, her introducing us to a whole new world of information. This special room had all kinds of pretty leather bound books on shelves against the wall, a high desk with a little chair in front of it, the top of the desk pulled down to make a flat surface, on the flat down surface part was a small glass bottle with dark black stuff in it. Misses called it "ink" that was used for writing, and laying beside it, a pretty feather with a very keen point which Misses Sarah called a "quill," that one looked like a turkey feather and there were others that looked like peacock feathers, she explained to us, "that this here room was where Masa John would sit and write letters to folks." She took a piece of paper, dipped the "quill" into the little bottle of black stuff she called "ink" and made some marking on some paper, showed them markings to us and said "they were our names, and soon we'd be able to do that for ourselves in the future." She did not let us keep the paper, thought we might make a mistake and show them to someone.

When we cleaned this room we always gently wiped the leather bound books like they were something special. The room had a special smell to it, like leather and the smell of brandy and cigars. Misses Sarah told us to do that, always adding, 'now ya'll be careful with all the things in this room, everything valuable you know!"

Misses Sarah told us she was going to teach us to read and write. When she told us that, the two of us just stood like we were frozen, not knowing what to say, so we say nothing.

She started us off in sometime called a "blue book speller" she would say the word and would have us repeat after her. That was easy to me, seems like just saying what somebody else had just said. She said if we missed any words she would make us run the mile to and back from the front door of the plantation to the entrance of the plantation carriage road to the house. We did not want that to happen.

I finally asked her myself, "Misses Sarah ain't you going against the law doing this?" I am! She replied. But the way I see it, times are changing in this United States. The government seems to be having a hard time deciding who is right in this slavery issue or as Missus called it "Our peculiar Institution." She said "when governments get to the point they cannot agree, that means trouble and sooner or later somebody is going to get mad and start fighting."

She continued talking as if we were not even in the room "I have heard Masa John and the other men talking about the situation, and they just don't know what is going to happen, but either way I made up in my mind you two girls needed to have some kind of education later on, plus teaching you both gives me something to do, all my children and Grand

children live somewhere else and after all who is going to tell it? You?"
"No ma'am" we said!"

"I'm not going to tell it either, so there!" Misses Sarah laughed, Rachael
and me didn't laugh, we didn't know whether to or not."

My Mama, Willie Mae and Rachael's mother knew what was going on,
and they were so scared, but they were not going to open their mouths.
We had told Grandma Anna, and she said" Lawd, Lawd, Lawd you done
heard by prayers that my chillums gonna be educated, thank you Lawd!
Thank you Jesus." Now you girls study real hard and learn all you can,
and keep your mouth shut about what Misses Sarah doing, you'll hear
me?" they treat her and you all mighty bad if'n they find it out what she
doing. We nodded our heads in agreement.

Of course the Bible was our main study book for learning, but there
were many others. Misses Sarah used slates and lined tablet paper and
taught us how to make slanted lines on the paper or the slate, had to stay
between the lines, could not let the pencil or chalk mark go above or
below the line. The slate was easier to use, cause Misses Sarah could rub
the marking off and use the board again and again. When she used the
paper she had to burn it so no one would see anything. If we got it wrong
on the slate she just erased and we have to do it again and again til we get
it right. Then she would show us words that had straight lines, again we
would mark the straight lines on the slate.

Next she started us on making circles, but the circles had to be slanted to
the right. Not below the line, not above the lines, just circles, in between
the lines, and the circles had to be connected. Day after day, month after
month, this teaching continued. Words began to take shape and had
names. I finally could write my name. I wrote my name "Lucy Mae."
It was written on paper between the lines and looked so pretty to me.
Misses Sarah so proud of her teaching and our learning. T'was the year
1856, Rachael, JB and me all be sixteen years old.

Misses Sarah said we need to know how to spell our colors, so she teach
us them like this:

She show us an apple, we say apple, she say "red", then write "red" on the slate, we have to copy "red" down. She show us another apple, we say apple, she say, "green", had to write "green". She did this with all the colors.

She take us out on the porch and tell us to look up, then ask us what we see, we answer: "sky" she say "blue". We follow her back inside and she write "blue", we copy "blue". This is how she teaches us, very slow and just a few things at a time. Misses know Grandma always tell us The Christmas Story. She said if we remember any word we do not know when Grandma Anna told us the "Christmas Story", save them in our head and we discuss them on the lessons that come later. "Yes sum", we answered.

Misses Sarah lessons to us continued. This time she started numbers, first we had to learn to count the number of fingers and toes we had. Then she made subtracting and multiplying like little games, using our fingers to pretend that we had cut off some of our fingers or toes, and count to see how many we had left, seemed crazy to me, but it worked and did we laugh! She so pleased with the progress Rachael and me making, then too, She pleased with herself too!

The Christmas Gift

About three weeks before any Christmas Grandma Anna would get started on telling all of us in the family "The Christmas Gift" story. It would take her about a week to tell it all. She liked making the story long. She would only go so far, and then she would say "go to bed chillum, tell you tomorrow more of it". This was the job she gave herself every Christmas season; she prided herself in being able to remember every word each year the preacher man said about the birth of Jesus. Grandma Anna named the story "The Christmas Gift".

Everyone would gather around the blazing fire in the hearth, before she begin, she would tell all the females to cover their legs with a quilt, because the heat from the fire in the hearth would cook your legs without you even feeling it. Leaving burns splits and cracks in the skin that would get infected. While she was telling the story, she would stop from time to time for us to turn around and warm our backsides, and wrap ourselves up again in quilts and sat down. That keep you warm for a little while.

This is how she told the story:

God sent one of his angels to talk to a young girl in Nazareth, which was a town in Galilee. This girl's name was Mary, she was maybe about fifteen or sixteen years old I guess. Like me and Rachael's age.

When the angel told her she would have a baby and the baby would be a boy who she must name "Jesus."

Well, Mary was so scared she did not know what to do, or who to turn too.

She asked him how this could happen, I am a virgin!

The angel went on to explain, "Do not be scared, this child would be the son of God."

My little brother Runt spoke out saying "Grandma why she be scared?"

"The angel scare her?"

Grandma Anna said "cause she was experiencing something strange and new to her, it be confusing to her son". She continued on with her storytelling, nothing Grandma Anna liked better than telling Bible stories. Grandma Anna good at telling bible stories, and wisdom stories, plus ghost stories too!

She said, Mary was gonna be married to a young man from her home town. His name Joseph. After Mary told him what the angel had said, he was confused and sort of angry with Mary.

He was building them a house to live in; he just lost interest and stopped. Poor Mary had told him the truth and she did not know what else to do.

Joseph still kept trying to figure out all he had heard her tell him.

After a while and angel came to Joseph and told him what God had planned for Mary, he also told Joseph the child must be named "Jesus," and not to do anything. Just wait for the birth and be the earthy father to Jesus, so Joseph did just that.

While they were waiting for Mary to have the baby, Caesar Augustus made a law everyone that lived in the territory under the control of Rome, had to go back where they was born and register to be counted.

Joseph took Mary and went to Bethlehem in Judea, cause his family line was from David, the King. "You all remember little David who killed that giant?" She did not wait for us to answer, just kept talking.

Grandma Anna said "the trip must have been horrible for Mary, cause she had to ride on a donkey over all that rocky road, bouncing all around. But poor Joseph had to walk all that way too. Runt (JW) said "I bet he be tired too".

"Yea, he was" she said, but Joseph tried to make it as easy on Mary as he could, but through it all she never complained.

There were folks from everywhere; you talk about crowded, so crowded there were no rooms open in the inns, which were places you could pay to stay in out of the elements.

Joseph told the inn keeper what was going on with him and Mary his wife. The innkeeper looked at Mary and knew they needed some where they could rest and lay their heads down. He told Joseph he had a stall where the animals were kept, the place might not have been the best and maybe not too clean, but it was dry and warm because of the animal's body heat.

Having no other choice Joseph took the offer and he and Mary went to the stall which was in a cave.

There were some shepherds that were watching over their sheep that night to keep wild animals from attacking them. While they were sitting and talking and watching some angels appeared singing and then told them what was going to happen that night.

They did not believe them, so the shepherds decided to go to Bethlehem to see for themselves. Everyone agreed "let's go!"

At that point she would say" enough for tonight, go to bed, will tell you more tomorrow night. We were not sleepy, so Grandma gave us some turkey foot soup to help us get to sleep.

Guess you are wondering by now how we always had so much turkey foot soup, some of it was also made from chicken feet, and we just called all of it "turkey foot soup."

The next night Grandma got us all settled in to take up where she left off on the Christmas story.

"You remember what I told you about the shepherds?" "Yes ma'am, we do!"

"Well, those shepherds saw the baby Jesus, and they just loved him, such a beautiful baby. Little baby laying there just stretching and yawning, looking around." They thanked Mary and Joseph for allowing them to see the baby, and then they returned to their job of watching the sheep. The two shepherds that had stayed and watched the sheep for the first group to go, left going to see what the others had already seen, I speck.

"Just like now chillum, news spreads, so other folks begin to talk about what had happened and this new King that had been born, folks called him Jesus."

There was a mean old King in office named Herod, crazy as a loon! He heard about this baby everybody was talking about, saying he was a king, cause by then Mary and Joseph had carried Jesus to the temple and other folks had seen him.

Well that crazy old Herod wrote a decree or law that said all boys four years and younger were to be killed. Thinking that this would rid him of this "JESUS."

Someone told Herod that some wise men were traveling through the area on their way to see Jesus. Herod sent for them and told them when they found the baby, well by that time Jesus was an older baby, but to come back and let him know, so he could go worship him too, he lied! He wanted him killed.

Those wise men were truly wise, after they saw the child, they gave him all kinds of precious gifts. They went back home a different way, but don't you know that crazy old Herod killed other boy babies!, didn't get Jesus though, an angel came and told Joseph to flee to Egypt and stay there until they came again to tell him news that Herod was died. You see the Lord's work must go on. No man is powerful enough to stop that. With this Grandma Anna ended the "Christmas Gift Story," like Christmas, it was stored away in her head until next Christmas.

Christmas Visits

Christmas time was a special time for everyone. We had become a little bit more knowledgeable because of Misses Sarah. She was still teaching, Rachael and me. Nobody has ever said anything cause they didn't know nothing about what Misses was doing! Grandma Anna always keep telling us, "don't talk no different, don't walk no different, don't put on no airs, just be the same Lucy Mae and Rachael ya'll is, you'll hears me?" "yes 'am!"

Christmas morning if weather was not too bad. After everyone had eaten, the visitation circle began.

Family that lived farthest away would leave home, walk to visit their neighbor. Nobody had anything to give like gifts, so the greeting from visitors would always be to each other, "Christmas Gift."

Whatever had been cooked at that house a little of it was eaten, then the two families would head off together to visit the next family. Something was eaten or drunk at each stop. This continued the entire day until every family would have left their home to visit the next house, like in a circle. Each family leaving with the entire group to visit another home, finally they arrived back to where the first family lived and where the visit had started.

As they reached each house, the families "good bye." That way nobody walked home alone . . . they circled the same way like they started until each family was back safely where they started from.

Visiting, eating, drinking, walking, talking, a good way to pass the holidays with family and friends, cause tomorrow if it was not Sunday, church going day, it was a work day for the slaves.

Moral of this story: Every day that God gives is a special day, no matter what happens.

To Catch a Hummingbird

The years passed in time for us just as they do for all people. Times changed, conditions did not, many Decembers have come and many have gone. The year is 1860, in our situation nothing had changed for us, except we had some learning. Lotta things going on though. Everybody "white" talking about "states rights," and "who gonna do what."

We, the grandchildren are getting older, but so was Grandma Anna, Grandpa Job, Willie (my Papa) and my Mama (Willie Mae).

When thinking about changes I sometimes shudder, wondering what the out come of all this will be, transitions are so final. Maybe our life's transitions, Rachael and me, would be for the better sooner or later.

All of us chillum were four years older, I am now twenty-one years old. "Runt" the baby was thirteen years old, that be hard to believe.

Grandma Anna still likes her plants and flowers. Down through the years she had always had someone or herself to dig up wild flowers to replant in her front yard flower garden. These flowers come back year after year, so all she had to do was to plant any new ones she ran across.

Just as tenderly as she would kissed us on our foreheads, that's the same tenderness she used when placing the wild flowers in the ground.

In the late spring and summer months you could see her rocking in her rocking chair watching bird and insects flying around her flower garden.

She loves the smell of honeysuckle vines, but she never planted them close to the cabin. She said "them honeysuckles would cover the whole cabin, dem plants are really wild, they run all the time, just like JB! Our community news bearer!

Her having so much knowledge of plants and wild flowers, she could name each of them and what they were used for in medicine: African Daisy, Baby's Breath, Queen Ann's Lace, Black eyed Susan, Catch fly, Chicory, Cone Flower, Bachelor's Button, Primrose, Lemon Mint, Sage, Wild Onions, Sweet Williams and many more, she taught me all the things she knew about these plants, what was dangerous and what was not dangerous.

Grandma Anna loved to watch the bird and butterflies come to the flowers.

My little brother JW "Runt" watched them too, but not for pleasure, he had something else in his mind, "catching a hummingbird."

"JW I see you eye balling them hummingbirds when they come around here, best you leave them birds alone" Grandma Anna said. JW never said a word back to her, just kept watching them birds like they had cast a spell on him.

I hear him talking to Andrew, told him "them birds look like bees darting here and there, back and fo so fast, and it would be fun to catch one to hold it still and get a good look at it." Andrew said to him, "you heard what Grandma Anna said" but "suit yourself."

That evening before Grandma Anna came outside, JW was already standing there at the flower bed staring at those fast moving little birds. Some of the flowers had long necks, they were called "trumpet flowers" the birds would go down into the tubs of them to get the sweet nectar. I told him, "Boy, Grandma Anna said to leave them birds alone, you hear her say so." He walled his eyes at me and said "mind your own business!" and so I did.

I guess his mind told him "ready! Set! Go!" While that bird was inside that flower he grabbed the whole flower with the bird inside. You guessed it! That bird bored a hole in his hand so fast, he dropped the flower, the little hummingbird zipped away like he was a drunk man. At first JW just stared at his bleeding hand, and then I guess his brain must have told him to holler! Out comes the rest of the family to see what had happened to him. I had seen what happened, so I told the others!

Grandma Anna said to me "Lucy Mae why didn't you stop him?" I answered, "he told me to mind my own business" so did, besides it happened too fast for me to tell him not to do it, so I just watched the fun take place."

Grandma Anna said "boy your head is as hard as a rock, I told you not to bother them birds."

Out comes the cold oil, to clean and bandage his hand. Know what? It was his right hand, and he is righted handed! What a mess that was! so much for using that hand for eating and what not's!

Now when the hummers come around, he goes inside. Grandma told him them hummers never forget who bothered them and they would always come after that person forever, poor JW. He believed her!

Don't care how hot it was, when the hummers came, he went inside!

Seems like being hard headed be like a cold, catching! Rachael's little brother had a bad habit of catching them big yellow and black bumble bees in the Holley hawk flowers. His Mama, Joyce had told him to stop that, did him? Naw!

Joyce told my mama Willie Mae, the Holley hawk flower was not strong enough to hold the bumble bee and "Baby Brother, which is what they called him," was not strong enough to handle the bumble bee.

Moral of this: Do hard heads stay hard forever, and if they do what are the end results?

Section V

Skunks

Remember that old hound dog Grandpa Job owned named Bottom? Think I have told you how lazy he was, just too lazy to grunt. Early one morning just at daybreak, he spotted something moving in the field across the road. Must have perked his curiosity, cause off he ran to see what it was. Found out real soon too, t'was a Momma skunk and three babies trotting behind her. Well Bottom started meddling and raising a ruckus, making that Mama skunk nervous, scared and mad, cause she was gonna protect those little babies of hers. Closer Bottom got, faster she stomped her feet to warn him "GET BACK" then all a sudden, she used the only weapon God had gave her for protection, "skunk spray!" She aimed right for that old hound dogs eyes with that liquid stinky skunk spray. Well, he backed up, howling, rolling in that dirt and grass in that field trying to get that scent off him. Well the first place he headed for was home and the cabin, justa looping and hollowing!

By that time Grandpa Job was already up. He had gone outside to get some eggs out of the hens nest out in the chicken coop to cook for us to eat. He heard Bottom, and saw him running! That dog, scent and all, headed right for Grandpa Job, well, we heard "get outta here, go way from here dog!" Over and over these words got louder and louder!

When that dog got closer Grandpa took the old walking stick of his and whipped him off. Well Bottom had never been whipped before and I am sure he was confused at Grandpa Job treating him that way. He turned, tucked his tail under him and ran under the cabin to his place by the chimney.

Everybody holding they noses! Grandpa Job threw that walking stick out in the yard. Left it there and used his spare. All of Bottom's food was thrown way out in the yard so he could not get near the house until the skunk smell left him. Took a long time though!

I am sure Bottom has spotted skunks since then, but to my knowledge has he ever taken that route again!

Pending Unrest

Eighteen sixty, things really buzzing about this thing over slavery. Misses Sarah said "everybody talking, nobody listening." She said "folks just be running their mouths." When she said that to us, us covered our mouths to keep her from seeing us laughing, she not pay us any attention, just kept fussing and talking.

Most folks have heard or somehow knew tempers had been getting hotter and hotter between the northern states and the southern states over "States rights," but we knew, we not crazy, or dumb, the whole issue was about folks like us and taking folks like us into the new territories and land the United States was getting.

Kansas and Nebraska seemed to giving, what they called "Congress" in Washington. DC fits. Seems like Congress had made a deal with some southern folks in Congress, and passed the Kansas-Nebraska Act, saying folks moving to these territories could carry their slaves with them into these areas and these colors still be slaves.

They was saying out in Kansas things had gotten so bad, so many folks for slavery spreading, and so many not for it spreading into the territories. Things got so bad that folks had start killing each other. Heard Masa say something about "Bleeding Kansas." Everybody talking, but us still going on about their daily business, not in our back yard yet!

Mockingbird, Mockingbird Sing Me a Song

When everyone had the chance to rest in the late afternoon. We would join Grandma outside the cabin to listen to some of her wisdom, or just to sit quietly.

We had a thicket little piece away from the cabin. In that thicket bush lived a mockingbird. Had lived there far as long as I could remember, if it was not him, was his kin, and they just keep using that same bush for their home. Grandma Anna said they can get real mean when they think you are gonna get near they nesting place." We went about our business, they went about theirs, and the two of us never crossed each other's paths, so to say. Had no reason to attack us.

Weather was so hot, all of us sitting outside before dark. Mockingbird setting on a limb in one of the trees, his tail bobbing up and down.

Grandma Anna said "watch this." She made several sounds, and then told us to make some sounds, then sit still and listen. We all made different sounds, then hushed and got real quite.

Little time passed, then all of a sudden that mockingbird was making the same sounds we had made, but they just sounded better!

We listened and laughed, but not too loud, so as not to spook him away or maybe cause him to stop.

When he would rest a spell, my brothers would make more sounds, then listen!

Mocking bird made the same sound.

Grandma Anna said the moral of this story was:

"Never say something you don't want repeated!" She said "Lucy Mae, Rachael, this lesson mean you, you'll learning a lot, thanks to Misses Sarah, but keep your mouths shut, don't change your talk, your walk or you actions, somebody will notice and quite a few folks be in big trouble, you two understand me?" Yes ma'am! She finished it off with this warning "Talk slowly, think fast." She keep telling us that same thing over and over like we don't understand the first time . . . I think maybe Grandma Anna be real scared for us. My Papa Willie say she just be getting old and repeating herself, I told him "no such thing, Grandma Anna got good mind."

Easter Time

Spring be a 'coming, Misses always like to decorated house for any special day, and this special day a 'coming be "Easter."

Big crowd of Masa John's friends came to stay for several days, they brought their wives and chillums with them, so the "big House" busy, busy just like Christmas time. JB who was twenty-one years old now same as me, had become a carriage driver, which meant he took care of the carriages and horses, he would drive Masa John and his friends places and would just listen to their conversations. In our spare time the three of us would get together and secretly talk about what we had heard.

Rachael and me had become house maids, which gave we access to the entire house, and folks behind walls do talk, and since we there, we do listen.

The women visitors brought their personal maids, and of course, the drivers for each of the carriages came. Masa John had built servants quarters for slave men and slave women who traveled wit their owners to his plantation to stay in while dey here.

Rachael and me cleaned them cabins from time to time. They called them "slaves visiting quarters." Grandpa and Andrew built the fires when fires were needed in them cabins where these colors gonna be staying.

Everyone greeting, laughing, talking, getting settled in. Mayor of Murfreesboro, Aaron Venable Brown and his wife, the Governor of the State of Tennessee and he family, folks in the Nashville government among the guest here, so we all knew we would hear a lot of stuff bout what be going on in other areas of the United States. After each meal men would go to Masa John's study for coffee, brandy liquor and conversation. Faster the brandy liquor worked, looser dem tongues came, no telling what gonna come outta they mouth.

Ladies would go into ladies sitting room. Every one of us looking at each other, saying with our eyes "keep your ears open." Ladies try to pretend they do not take nips of whiskey, but they do! A few drops in coffee or tea, and they were discussed everything you could think of! Colored help gotten laugh off that!

Did not have to wait long for talking to start, seems like up north some folks had started a new political party called "Republicans."

Masa John's group of men were discussing bout what happened in 1857. This traveling Doctor had carried his slave named Dred Scott into the new territory of Kansas to help him with his doctoring. The Doctor and Dred Scott petitioned the Federal Government to declare Dred Scott his freedom, cause that area was not slave territory at that time, the Court said "no," so Scott remained a slave. Folks up north, they say, got real upset about this. One of the visiting men said that "later on Scott bought his, his wife and his daughter's freedom," with the help of his Doctor, now his ex-owner.

Look like we had a lot of catching up to do on the news on slavery. The slaves that came with their owners to visit Masa John, begin to join in the secret talk with us telling us what they had heard. They say, they heard they Masa's talking about in 1859, this person names John Brown, who had most white folks thinking he was crazy and wishing he would keep his mouth shut. This Mr. John Brown had gotten so tired of slavery till he decided to try and take matters into his own hands. He planned and carried out a raid at Harper's Ferry, Virginia. He be defeated in what he tried to do, so they gave him a trial, found him guilty and they hanged him. Folks that was for him made up a song 'bout him, singing "John Brown body lays a molding in his grave, but his cause be marching on," we heard colored folks added those last lines."

Next day be Sunday, Easter Sunday! Me, Rachael, Joyce and Willie Mae, my Momma, been up all night boiling grasses, using dried flowers, dandelions, wood chips, berries and whatever else kind of plant that would color the water for dying the boiled eggs for hunting today.

Older cooks in the kitchen cooking up Easter breakfast right along with Easter dinner, Ham being the main dish, and of course mashed potatoes with sweet pickles and eggs mashed into a type tasty dish. Anything you think you wanted to eat they pretty much had cooked that too!

Visiting slave maids had to bath them white chillum, get them ready for looking pretty for church first, everybody white would eat dinner when we get back, then the egg hunt. Nobody walking to church today, white folks be in carriages, slaves be on wagons driven by black overseers. Guess white overseers having themselves a good old holiday. Some slaves had to remain at the plantation: cooks, some of the maids who set the tables and did other chores. Some of the men who were house servants remained at the plantation, but we got lucky, we got to go to church, taw's a change. Lawd! Lawd! A little rest!

Easter time when slaves get new sets of clothes too, so everybody was dressed up going to First Baptist Church to hear preacher man tell about how Jesus had raised himself from the dead on this special day. He told us about the three women, the two Mary's one the Mother of Jesus and the other Mary, coming to the tomb to rub the spices and oils Nicodemus had given to use on preparing Jesus body. Pastor say the women found the tomb empty. Jesus not be there just like he had said about himself. Women so scared, they saw a man who they thought was the grounds keeper, and asked him where the body was. Well, the grounds keeper was really an angel. He told him Jesus was alive again and to go tell the others. They left running to tell the others what had happened.

We finally arrived at church. We settle down in our places in the balconies to wait for service to start. Good part about that balcony, you can see everybody coming and going. Little white girls and those in their teens as well, coming in all prettied up, buckled shoes, pretty dresses made by the slave seamstresses, who did nothing but make clothes, if it be a man slave doing this type of work, he be called a tailor, by trade.

All the house guest we had went to church with us today at First Baptist. Pastor made a special afford to welcome everyone and especially Masa John's guest, cause they were the most important folks in the state of Tennessee government.

Pastor don't make sermon very long cause he too want to enjoy beautiful Easter weather and his Misses and chillum wanted to hunt eggs.

After the Easter eggs hunt chillums are tired and sleepy, fretful, and just not in a good mood like chillum get when they tired, so they Mama's turned them over to their slave maids servants to bath, rock and put them to bed.

JB and the other carriages drivers be cleaning the carriages, shinning the parts that could be shined, and cleaning out the insides. Others be caring for the horses, grooming them, get them ready to turn out to pasture so they can rest for the long trip tomorrow morning back to Nashville.

Clarence, one of the visiting slave carriage drivers, began telling the others about a book that seemed to be causing a big problem on the issues of slavery, states rights, and succession. He and Nick, another slave horse groomer, told JB and the others listening about a book that had been written and published in 1852.

The book be called "Uncle Tom's Cabin," the writer name be a Miss Harriet Beecher Stowe. She lived up north, so they say, but had listened to all the stories freed and escaped slaves had told her. They say Harriet Tubman had even talked with her, telling her about the horrible conditions us faced daily. They say Miss Harriett's Daddy be against slavery too.

She tell about things we already know about though, cause we live them things every day. White folks that read that book, some of them got mad as a hornets nest that had been knocked down.

Nick say he heard one of his Masa's friends talking bout what President Lincoln say when he meet Miss Harriet Beecher Stowe, they say he say, "so you the little lady that caused this big war!" They say she say, "no Sir Mr. Lincoln, slavery be the cause for that when it come!"

You see, that new Republican Party that was formed ran Mr. Lincoln for President. Mr. Lincoln be from Springfield, Ill. When election count be over Mr. Lincoln was the winner, that was November 1860. Clarence added that white folks that in favor of slavery, state's rights and other stuff, not pleased at all.

Seems like South Carolina got so upset she succeeded from the union, that is, "she say she no long a part of the United States of America." Everybody laughed about that. How you gonna break away from something you still a part of? can't take your land and move it somewhere else.

Overseers be about ready to make their rounds, checking on plantation slaves at Cedar Grove that had not left for home, which was Bethel. Specially fo dark, they always pay close attention to the slaves that be clustered around talking. Think we be planning something, but to tell the truth we be listening to all the news we can get, that news one day may be useful to us.

JB say, when overseers see too many slaves gathering talking, they began to make their rounds. They thinking and wondering why after all the chores be finished why slaves still be at Cedar Grove and not heading home to Bethel? When JB and the others see them coming, they bid each other good bye and hit the road toward Bethel. White overseer sit on his horse and watch them leave.

Female's maids that worked at the plantation, like Rachael and me and some others had to get everyone settled in for the night, after that, then we go to the kitchen to help Mama, Joyce and the other kitchen folks finish so we all could head for home. Be dark but you bet your bottom dollar an overseer be right behind you riding and watching.

Grandma's Late Easter Surprise

When we get close to the cabin, we smell something that smell really good. My brothers, who were with the males that left for Bethel earlier were sitting outside resting, but they had smelled those good smells too.

I asked Ruben, "what Grandma Anna cooking?" He say "a surprise for all us."

Going inside we hugged my Grandparents, something that most slaves do, seeing as how it might be the last time we see each other. So we hug when we leave and we hug when we come back.

Grandma Anna had made "T cookies" some folk's call them "sugar cookies" and some good hot spiced mint tea, and these were the Easter surprise for all us who had to work all that day.

Next morning at Cedar Grove everybody getting ready to head back to Nashville.

Kissing, hugging, handshaking, going on between everybody. Visiting slaves and the slaves at Cedar Grove acted like we not know each other, that action be best for us, so we just nod our head good-bye to everyone.

After everybody gone things at Cedar Grove began to get back to normal.

JB and me be the same age, twenty-one years old, we still friends too, and when we have time, we talk about a lot of things.

He asked me had I ever thought about getting married to anyone. I say to him "I don't know JB, gotta wait it out and see how things turn out for us slaves later on."

How about you? I asked, "Pretty much the same feelings as you I guess."

I guess this big war Pastor Merry talked about when he be here, soon be coming our way. I hear them Northern army officers heading closer and closer to Nashville and I guess Murfreesboro soon too. Maybe I can volunteer to be a soldier, and fight, might make me a free man later on.

"Only thing worry me Lucy Mae, I can't read or write, that be a hindrance when you a freeman, unless you get something special you can do to make a living, what can I do? I just a silly little old slave boy when I were younger working them bacca fields. Now I drive a carriage for Masa, but that don't take much sense to do that, just gotta keep the carriage in the road, that be all."

"Don't feel that way about yourself JB, You worked with the horses, breaking, riding, grooming and taking care of them, and you know how folks in Tennessee feel about them "walking horses" why you think you can't do that kind of work?" "Don't know Lucy Mae what lay in store for me, just have to wait and see, bit by bit maybe it all fall into place, might have to join the soldiers fighting in this here war we is having, just don't know! If Federal troops come through here, kinda have already made up my mind I gonna go wit them, life might be hard when I join them, but I just wanna be free to go where I want, when I want, and come back when I please, without the right to do that Lucy Mae, seems like life not worth very much, not even worth living." I looked at JB very hard and said to him "JB let's just pray that whatever you do will be best for you, alright?" We both sat silently, just thinking to ourselves.

The Resurrection and ASK

One day just out of the clear blue sky, Runt says to me, "Lucy Mae, how did Jesus die on the cross, get buried in a tomb or grave, then come back to life again and his disciples and lots of other folk saw him?"

For a minute I was completely caught off guard and just stood there silently, not knowing just quite what to say to him.

"Well Runt I don't know if I am really the one to explain that to you, but I know someone who can," we both say "Grandma Anna."

Later that night when everyone was pretty must settled down, I said to Runt "Runt ask Grandma Anna all the questions you ask me this morning." He did just that, repeating word for word everything he had asked me, adding even more questions than those he had already asked. "Grandma Anna how we know that Jesus arose from the grave like Pastor Singleton says, what is resurrection, how we know for sure these things happened?"

His questions did not seem to come as a surprise to Grandma Anna. She sat there quietly for a while, and finally she said to Runt "I am going to tell you two things that happen that should make it kind of clear to you. Then I will give you a fact from the Bible that pulls it all together.

"Birth, living, death, dying, mercy, grace, and salvation are all fitted together into one process for us as humans. We all must have something called "faith," that faith must be in Jesus Christ. We must believe that Jesus lived, died and lived again."

"When you Grandpa Job get ready to plant beans he puts the bean in the ground, pretty soon the shell of that beans pops open, the shell decays or rots away but the inside of that bean begins to grow, sprout, and something else living comes out of it.

Pretty soon a new plant that looks completely different from the bean he planted peeps up out of the ground. That be like the resurrection son, the important part never dies. That is just the way God works son, he has placed within us a part of himself that never dies. This Son is called the Holy Spirit."

"The next thing I'm going to tell you about I will need you to help me with it, is that alright with you?" He answered "yes sum."

"Let's pretend your foot is the soul of Jesus, and your shoe is the body of Jesus where the (soul, spirit) breath lives."

"Jesus did go to the cross, hanged there and died, but before he died, he said, "Father I commit my spirit back into your hands," and immediately, the breath that God had breathed into Jesus that made him alive went back to God." "Take your foot out your shoe! Where your foot?" "Right here!" "Where the shoe?" "Right there." Is the shoe moving? "no mam" "why not?" "cause my foot not in it," "right" she answered. "Now, put your foot back in your shoe, "yes mam," "can you move your shoe?" "yes mam" "Why?" "Cause something living is in my shoe, my foot and my leg came back in my shoe."

"Now that's just the way God wanted it to be, Jesus's body lay right there waiting for God to send his spirit and breath back into him, and he did, and Jesus arose again alive."

"Runt, there is something the bible teaches us all that we must have, and that son is called "FAITH," faith is belief, a belief in something that we know is true, but we cannot see it. Like Grandma Anna loves you, but can you see the love?" "No mam," but that does not change the fact that you know it and believe it does it?" "no' mam."

Now faith is being sure of what we hope for and certain of what we do not see. Now let's talk about faith Runt, and all these folks I'm gonna tell you ok?"

Hebrews 11:1 says:

By faith Abraham offered Isaac as a sacrifice

By faith Isaac blessed Jacob and Esau

By faith Jacob blessed Joseph's sons when he was dying

By faith Joseph spoke to the children about them leaving Egypt

By faith Joseph told the people what to do with his bones after his death

By faith Moses mother hid him for three months when he was a baby

By faith Moses parents were not afraid of the King's command to kill all boy babies

By faith Moses refused to be called the son of Pharaoh's daughter

By faith Moses left Egypt

By faith Moses was the first to keep the Passover Feast

By faith the people passed through the Red Sea

By faith walls of Jericho fall down

By faith Rahab the prostitute kept the spies safe from harm

By faith the family of Rahab was not killed

By faith Gideon defeated the Midianites

By faith Barak "lighting" obeyed the Judge Deborah and defeated the Cananites

By faith Samson brought down the temple of the Philistines with his strength

By faith Jephthah defeated the Ammonites

By faith David ruled Israel and Killed Goliath

By faith Samuel was a prophet and judge, he anointed Saul and David as Kings of Israel

By faith Daniel went into the Lion's Den

By faith Jonah lived in the belly of a great fish for three days

By faith Saul becomes Paul and serves Jesus in his missions of starting churches

By faith the prophets served God

By faith the Disciples followed Jesus Christ

By faith in God Jesus went to the cross

By faith what will you do?

Grandma Anna ended her lesson on faith with a question to us. Any other questions Runt? "yes sum" he said. "Go ahead and ask me Baby boy." You say, "God know what you gonna say foe you say it?" "Yes He do," if He know then why I gotta ask?" She answered him, "cause God like for you to talk to him." "Spose all us here in this here cabin not talk to you", how you feel then? He said "sad!" so . . . Runt after all the things God do for us, he too would be sad if in we not talk to him and thank Him. "He be mad?" Grandma Anna laughed "No Baby, not mad just sad."

Sitting in her rocking chair she began to hum and sing:

> Hush, Hush, somebody's calling my name
> Hush, Hush, somebody's calling my name
> Hush, Hush, somebody's calling my name
> Oh my Lawd, Oh my Lawd what shall I do?
> Sounds like Jesus that be calling my name
> Sounds like Jesus that be calling my name
> Oh my Lawd, oh my Lawd what shall I do?

Rocking back and forth in her rocking chair the words drifting into a hum, the hum drifting slowly away, but the rocking continued. We knew this was her private time with God, so we said nothing else, we just left, giving her private meditation time.

Moral of this lesson: Believe! Faith is the key to the kingdom.

Emancipation Proclamation

January 2, 1862 President Lincoln issued something called the "Emancipation Proclamation." That piece of paper said any state that had slavery and was fighting against the union (those states that did not succeed) all the slaves as of that date in those states was free!

What us did not know at that time, was that Tennessee was not included in that law. The Federal officers and President Lincoln had already decided that before that law was issued that Tennessee was no long a battleground in rebellion against the Union. We will hear that later.

Everybody colored glad to hear the news, us celebrating, jumping up and down, crying, and screaming for joy. To test the law out some folks walked away from the plantation to see if anyone come looking for them, nobody did!

Free? Yes free! But free to do what? Free to go where? Free colors living in Murfreesboro did not have to decide this. They were already established in whatever skill they had and was making a living with. Many of them scared though I am sure, didn't know and could not imagine what's gonna happen in they cases 'fore this war ends.

Was January, folks living off what they had canned, dried and preserved.

No one on Cedar Grove ran away, we just waited to see what would happen.

Masa John called all the ex-slaves to the big house so he could talk to us. He explained the situation to everyone and told us how rough it might get later on. He told us we were free to stay or free to go, whatever was our choice. He explained to us that we were welcome to stay and any work we did would be for pay, but money would be tight, cause the South had started using money issued by the Confederacy, which he said would soon not be worth its own weight.

Masa John said, "folks could let him know what they decided to do after they had talked it over among themselves." Grandma Anna and Grandpa Job were now seventy-four years old. What do they do? The family had to consider their welfare. Willie was their only son, and in our traditions we have always been taught that the oldest son looks after his parents when they get old. My Pa's decision will affect other people other than him and my Mama. His decision was to remain right where he was. My Mama, Willie Mae was a good cook, she decided that she and Grandma Anna would began baking. Selling what was baked to those who wished to buy the baked goods.

Section VI

Captured

July 13, 1862 Nathan Bedfort Forrest and his troops were camped at Woodbury, Tennessee. He got word that the union troops had planned to pass through Murfreesboro, capture it and head for Chattanooga. Their aim was to capture and gain control of the railroads. When Forrest heard about these plans he and his troops left Woodbury, coming down Woodbury pike, which turned into Main Street when you got to Murfreesboro.

Some union troops were around the courthouse, shots were exchanged, union troops were caught off guard and scattered. Captured and became prisoners.

After that battle, Forrest heads for Oakland mansion, where more union troops were. Between being unprepared and the confusion that followed, the union officer Col. William Duffield surrender to Forrest. The surrender between the two officers took place inside the Maney House (Oakland Plantation) that same day.

Joining the Union Troops

My three brothers and JB decided to go join up with and follow the union troops. Some troops were camped near Stones River, they found their way to that location. We later heard that the camp was overrun with ex-slave, volunteers, whole slave families, old folks, and those following kin that had decided to follow the army. Conditions were terrible. We later learned my brothers and JB had joined up with the Second United States Infantry Regiment which later became the Thirteenth Regiment, United States Colored Troops so we heard.

They really did not get to see much fighting actions. Most of them were laborers, cooking, cleaning, and looking after white officers, digging trenches, guarding and repairing railroads, washing, ironing clothes and whatever, but not fighting at that time. Later on they would be called on the fight.

Seems to me like before January, in July and August it be too hot to fight anyway. Confederate troops walking the streets of Murfreesboro. Pretty uniforms on, tipping their hats to the ladies of the city. Nobody dreamed of what January would bring.

Things had not been torn up and everybody satisfied the war would be over in about a month or less. Plenty parties held in the fancy plantation homes for officers of the Confederate army.

Young single Murfreesboro young ladies hoping to meet a special young man from another area to strike a fancy for.

November and December come around, Misses Sarah still teaching Rachael and me. What she did not know, but our family did, was that Rachael had started teaching her brothers and sisters, and me my brothers.

Masa John had friends visiting him all the time now. Guess they discussing the war issues, when and if things would cause problems for Murfreesboro?

Troops be coming through taking whatever was not tied down, hauled off sheds and cabins they tore down for fire wood.

Crops not growing in winter, folks only had stuff they had canned and cured, even those were begged for and sometimes just taken.

No supplies coming in from up north for the union troops to feed they men.

Many times see a confederate or union solider come up to the cabin asking for food and water, cause we had nothing to give them, can't give what you do not have. Some of the soldiers figure we be lying and try to get rough wit us.

Masa John called all the slaves at Cedar Grove plantation to the big house. He explained the situation to all of us. Told us the meaning of President Lincoln's decree, they free to leave. Food was scarce, and he did not know how long this would last. He ask each person what they decide to do.

My Pa Willie told Masa John his deciding to stay and look after his family. Masa John told him he would be fair to them.

January of 1863 things not any more settled, if anything they seen to be getting worse.

Misses Sarah and some of the other white First Baptist church ladies decided to ask white and colored females to go and help them doctors take care all the soldiers that be suffering and needed help. Masas Sarah took charge of the whole business, these are the colored females that went to help from the Bethel community: Carolyn Carney, Flora Hall, Rowena Gannaway, Lucy January, Kitty Jordan, Sophia Thompson, Judy Wendell,

Dorkas Miller and Cornelia Gentry. Wit all the suffering and dying that be going on they loaded up wagons with as many things as they thought the doctors that was running out of supplies might need. First Baptist Church on Sevier Street was used as a hospital. Things needed were, quilts, bandages, salves, whiskey, Grandma Anna's medicines and anything else they could use to care for the troops. Misses Sarah loads up me, Rachael, Willie Mae, some of the younger slave boys. Out of the house comes Grandma Anna! "Yall not going without me! Where my medicines go, I go!"

Mama tried to talk her out of it. She refused to move from in front of the wagon. Some of the younger boys helped her into the wagon, and away we went.

Finally arriving at the church. Conditions were terrible, the already freezing cold just added to the misery. Everyone went inside, Grandma Anna drew her breath in and placed her hand over her mouth, she was not prepared to see what she was seeing, and neither were we.

The church had been cleared of all the pews and any standing furniture that was in the way. The organ and its pipes were still in tack. Cots and pallets were placed everywhere. The place smelled like old urine, human waste, blood and vomit. Moaning, groaning, and screaming from the mouths of those having surgery, and it being done without the patient being knocked out, that's what the whiskey was used for, to knock them out. Wounded soldiers asking for help from anyone. Doctors who had run out of supplies and patience looked what they be! Weary! Worn! And tired!

Wagons were constantly rolling in from the battle fields, those who could not find a place at First Baptist, were carried over to Bradley Academy which was being used as a hospital too. The numbers seemed to be growing by leaps and bounds. Many families that knew where their loved ones was fighting hitched up the family wagon and followed the fighting from place to place, just in case their loved one was killed or injured they were there to see after them, or carry them home for burial if'n that be the case. There were no cemeteries, when folks died white or colored they be buried on the grounds of the plantation where they lived. There was a spot of ground located out on Church Street heads toward Shelbyville that colored folks had started using to bury they loved ones. The name of the cemetery was "Benevolent."

There were so many died, wagons with those needing to be buried and no one to take them home, passing each other a coming and a going to Benevolent Cemetery

Grandma Anna got busy, like we all did, bathing, dressing wounds, cooking food in the pots on the fires burning outside, feeding, and talking to those who wanted to talk to someone. We built small bucket fires to place close to the cots for much need heat for the soldiers, we heated bricks and rocks, wrapping them in blankets, placing them close to the soldiers who were shivering cold.

The food we cooked and served be Southern Hopping John, least that be what some folks called it. Most folks had plenty dried peas saved from the summer gardens, so that be no problem. The hopping john cooked up like soup, easy for hurt and sick folks both to eat as well as well folks.

Dried black-eyed peas
Water
Bacon or bacon fat or salt pork
Onions
Garlic (Grandma Anna had plenty of garlic)
Rice, if you had some, if not just the peas would do

I was amazed at how young the soldiers were, dey just mere boys!

I looks over toward the area where Grandma Anna was, she was sitting beside the bed of a young white confederate soldier, holding his hand, stroking it lovingly, rubbing his hands to warm them, softly whispering words of comfort. I very quickly looked away when she turned to reach for a hot wet cloth in a basin to wipe his face.

We worked all day and into the night by lanterns. We returned home late into the night, no one said much, and Grandma Anna said nothing. Just quietness and the rumble of the wagon wheels rolling and the horses tramping over the frozen dirt road!

That night before we went to bed, she looked at me and said "he is somebody's child," nothing followed that statement, only quietness again." Before laying down she kissed all of us, and you know where, right in the middle of our foreheads, "Good nite chillums."

Ending

All this final confusion came to an end with the surrender of the Confederacy to the Union in 1865. This horrible war had lasted from December 31, 1862 to January 2-13, 1865. When this was ended I was twenty six years old, the year was 1865.

The main Generals heading up of all this past confusion and killing of thousands, finally came to an end and met at Appomatox Courthouse, Virginia in the Mc Cellen home. General Robert E. Lee, spick and span in a brand new uniform, so it was said, and in contrast to the shabby private uniform Ulysses Grant was wearing. Side arms (guns) were kept by both sides. Southern soldiers were allowed to keep their horses and mules cause planting season which would soon be coming.

Took from then to April 1877 until all the federal troops left southern territory.

There's that number twelve again! It took twelve years for them to leave the south.

That's when "Reconstruction" begin. Reconstruction of property and lives, all things would never be the same, some folks handled it well, and others did not.

Folks from the north called "carpetbaggers" flooded the southern territory. Some came to help, others came to help themselves and to take advantage of a terrible situation.

"Carpetbaggers" were called that because folks said they had all they owned in them little bags that looked like the rugs on the floor in Masa John's study.

Schools for newly liberated slaves to learn to read and write were opened. Classes were held at First Baptist Church and Bradley Academy. Misses Sarah insisted that Rachael and me attend. She got us in the school. The teacher was Mrs. Dunlap. When she realized Rachael and me could read and write we were put in teachers positions. All my family attended the classes. Grandma Anna and Grandpa Job were eager to learn.

The year is now 1869, lots of things have come and gone. The Concord Association of which white First Baptist church was a part of held its annual convention and suggested that the colors of First Baptist Church be given the church and the property it was sitting on forever.

Down through the years until 1879 the Negros was allowed to pay what they could on the cost of the church. This lasted for a total of ten years.

I enrolled in school at the University for colored founded in 1866 in Nashville Tennessee, so did Rachael. We were 27 years old, seemed like marriage be far from our minds. We both completed our education and moved to the upper East coast of the Unites States. We both had turned thirty one years old. I became a professor (Doctor's Degree) at a prestigious university, teaching English and Literature. Rachael became a lawyer. She received several degree.

She said that she become a lawyer, that tirelessly, thankless, sometimes dangerous work for the cause of racial improvements for colors. By that time the NAACP had been formed, she became very active as a lawyer representing the NAACP in many cases.

Andrew became an educator. Ruben became our preacher and "Runt" becomes our medical Doctor graduating from MeHarry Medical School in Nashville, Tennessee.

My Mama and Daddy managed to buy the land our cabin was on, and several acres of land for our home place. Family reunions became a tradition for us.

Saying Farewell

Between 1870 and 1882 I made two trips back to Murfreesboro, one for Grandpa Job to be laid to rest (1870), the other for Grandma Anna's transition (1882). They both were carried into First Baptist Church on Spring and Sevier Streets for their funerals. In 1870 the pastor of First Baptist was Rev. Napolean Bonapart Frierson, he had been baptized by Rev. Merry. Rev. Frierson was 49 years old, his wife's name was Phobe, and she was 44 years old. They had three children, Napoleon Jr., Henry and John. Pastor Frierson died while being pastor of the church in 1872. Rev. Davis who had been the Pastor for the last ten years did the eulogy for Grandma Anna. These were the hardest things I've ever had to face in my life.

I sat with my brothers, their wives, children, we had grown in numbers in this family over the years. What a legacy Grandma Anna had left. My heart was heavy with sorrow, and seemed as if the tears would not stop falling. I cried out of love and respect for the greatest woman I have ever known.

My life of forty-four years has been an amazing journey of living, learning, loving and at times, anger, crying, and hating but through it all at the feet of one special lady called "Grandma Anna" I learned to endure. The one enduring force that will never change is "Love." It comes from God and God is eternal. I would like to share the three traditions that I learned as a little girl that still is an important part of the lives of my family, they are called "traditions," read, enjoy and remember.

Traditions

Having Strength
Being Tender
Keeping Faith

Grandma Anna's Granddaughter
Lucy Mae Mathis